W. James
4/12/11

WINGS
OF
GOLD

WINGS
OF
GOLD

•

J. P. MATHEWS

AVALON BOOKS
THOMAS BOUREGY AND COMPANY, INC.
401 LAFAYETTE STREET
NEW YORK, NEW YORK 10003

PRINTED IN THE UNITED STATES OF AMERICA
ON ACID-FREE PAPER
BY HADDON CRAFTSMEN, SCRANTON, PENNSYLVANIA

For all who serve,
and all who have served

Acknowledgments

Captain Niles R. "White Fang" Gooding, Jr., USN (Ret.),
former Commander Training Air Wing One, Naval Air Station,
Meridian, Mississippi, generously provided technical information,
advice, and review about the Naval aviation training process.

Linda Dunlap, Judith Alamia, and Dean Warren provided
invaluable editorial suggestions and assistance in the completion
of this book, without which it would not have been possible.

Regina Svendsen Mathews provided the patient support which
enabled it to be successful.

J. P. M.
Winter Springs, Florida
June 1995

Chapter One

"Sierra Papa Six, this is Red Barn. How do you copy? Over."

The radio message rasped through Navy Ensign Allison "Chip" Douglas's flight helmet. Gusty winds buffeted her T2-C jet trainer high above the Gulf of Mexico, a more serious distraction to her first solo landing at sea. "Red Barn" was the aircraft carrier *Forrestal,* miles ahead and five thousand feet below. Her career, even her life, depended on the next forty-five seconds.

"Red Barn, this is Sierra Papa Six," she answered. "I read you five by five."

The radio check verified the carrier's clear communication with her. If the ship's weather people had detected the strong wind gusts, they'd probably want to divert her into Pensacola and make her land on a safe concrete runway, instead of the carrier's now-pitching deck amid treacherous winds.

Not now, she pleaded silently. *Not after all this. Eighteen months of hard work, and I'm the only woman left in the class of five who started.* She'd practiced FCLP, or field carrier landings, on shore-based runways a hundred times. Carrier landings at sea were what she'd trained for all that time. Allison vectored the twin-engined airplane in a sweeping arc to her left toward final approach.

The carrier deck, three football fields long, seemed enormous when she'd walked it last night. The eighty-thousand-ton ship now looked like a postage stamp in the blue Gulf.

A failed carrier landing could mean death and the destruction of a multimillion-dollar airplane. She'd heard these landings described as the most intricate ballet in all of aviation. Five of them were required for qualification for flight students who sought their wings. And she was all too aware that some of the male pilots who waited below to evaluate her performance believed women weren't meant to be naval aviators.

Clear air turbulence bounced the white and orange training jet in bone-jarring jolts despite the sunlit sky. Allison wasn't certain her decision to land aboard was the best one, only that it was difficult and that she could do it. The turbulence would probably diminish at lower altitude. Then all she'd need worry about was a moving flight deck.

"Sierra Papa Six, advise if turbulence your location precludes safe approach to Red Barn. Bingo field is Pensacola, at heading 030, estimated flight time two zero minutes. Over."

The carrier *did* want her to consider waving off. She couldn't blame the Navy for not wanting to risk student pilots or aircraft on training flights. She must decide now.

In a voice she hoped did not waver, she replied, "Red Barn, this is Sierra Papa Six. Negative your last. I am turning on final and prepared to come aboard. Out."

If she waved herself off, the act would follow her forever. Macho male pilots would mock her. Her service reputation would matter years from now. If the Air Operations Officer or someone else ordered her to land on "the beach," that became their responsibility. She wouldn't make it easy for them.

The slender, raven-haired twenty-four-year-old with the soft voice and piercing hazel eyes had fought hard with naval aviation's male-dominated establishment to come this far. Today she'd remind them she was "Doug" Douglas's kid. Her father, a retired master chief petty officer and one of the Navy's few enlisted aviation pilots, had for years been a legendary character throughout the United States Atlantic Fleet.

The wide arc of flight brought her to the glide path. Beneath and ahead of her on the stern of the ship five miles ahead shone the bright ''meatball'' of the carrier's optical landing system, which would guide her down. Buffeting turbulence demanded intense concentration. Her eyes darted between the meatball and her instrument panel, tightly focusing every lesson of a year and a half into a few seconds. As a fleet pilot, she would have to land aboard during worse conditions than this, even at night in driving rain. And, she told herself, she would do it now. Perspiration made her face cool.

''Sierra Papa Six, this is Red Barn. How copy? Over.''

She recognized the gruff bark of Commander Pete Korinthos, the ship's air operations officer—the ''Air Boss.'' She hadn't taken their polite hint. Now they'd *order* her to divert, she thought.

''Not this time, boys,'' she muttered under her breath, eyes fixed on the rapidly unwinding altimeter. Gusty winds belted her plane unmercifully.

''This is Sierra Papa Six, ball, fuel state 1.2,'' she said, shorthand that she had acquired the optical landing system meatball and had an ample twelve hundred pounds of fuel remaining.

''Roger, ball,'' interrupted the landing signal officer, or LSO, on the same radio net, who acknowledged that she was on the way in. The LSO's transmission had blocked out what Korinthos was ready to say.

She would do it as her father had done it—the hard way. A few seconds later, she was close enough to see the wind-blown LSO, standing to the left of where she would touch down, his legs apart. Only his waveoff could stop her now, make her go around again, or divert. *I've done everything they taught me,* she thought. A trickle of sweat rolled down her brow and into her right eye, instantly stinging. She blinked, forcing both eyes wide open.

Her jet roared past the stern ramp of the carrier. Tons of metal thundered onto the armored steel deck amid squealing tires and roaring engines as she pushed her throttles forward. If she missed the wire, she'd need full power to take off again. The aircraft's massive tempered-steel tailhook seized the third flight deck wire with a resounding *clunk*. Allison lurched forward into the thick nylon harness that strapped her to the seat, yanking her throttles back as the hook engaged. The aircraft slowed from a hundred and twenty miles an hour to zero in three and a half seconds, the screaming engine tamed to a whisper now.

Underarms clammy, her face wet, Allison had brought her airplane home. As she rubbed a towel across her face, she recalled what aviators said about each carrier landing being a controlled crash.

The green-shirted flight deck crewman who directed her to park the aircraft smiled and nodded. He held up both hands, one with a thumb up, the other showing three fingers. She'd caught the third of the five landing wires, a perfect "trap." A thrill ran up her back. Five of the six aircraft behind her in the pattern had diverted into the Naval Air Station at Pensacola, Florida.

Minutes later, Commander Korinthos, his full face red, lips thin and tight, charged across the large wardroom toward her. He had stormed down from the ship's bridge once the last student was back aboard. The Air Boss would have lots to explain if Allison had slammed into the flight deck ramp or missed the wires with inadequate power and plunged into the sea. With several other flight students standing nearby, Korinthos seemed ready to ignore the Navy tradition of giving praise in public but censure in private. She'd expected something like this.

"Douglas, your perfect landing with those wind gusts and turbulence was beautiful but dumb!" he roared as he approached her. "Lousy judgment! Student pilots kill themselves trying to be hotshots. I would have waved you off if I thought you didn't have enough brains to do that yourself. Are you trying to prove something, Douglas? Answer me!''

Korinthos' face moved closer to hers, reminding her of relentless Marine drill sergeants in aviation officer candidate school. Her psyche had been further insulated against intimidation by that experience. She took another sip from her cup of tea before replying.

''Commander, if I can't land a Navy airplane anywhere in any weather, I don't deserve wings.'' Her voice was calm. ''You didn't order me to divert. The LSO didn't wave me off, I didn't blow any tires, and''—she hesitated—''it *was* a third wire trap . . . sir.'' She stifled the temptation to shrug.

The Air Boss's expression changed, his eyes narrowed. Korinthos mustn't have expected her unyielding answer.

''Third wire traps are luck, Douglas. Officers get paid for judgment. Aviators who live long enough to be Air Boss don't take dumb chances like that. The Navy can't spare any airplanes, or pilots, to satisfy big egos. Your father wouldn't have done that. Do you understand?'' His face moved closer again. His anger was no act, she thought.

''Yes, sir, I understand. But I know my father better than you do . . . sir.'' Korinthos never expected her to make another carrier landing after graduation, she thought. He must believe they'd put her in transports, helicopters, or some other Mickey Mouse aircraft that never landed on a carrier—and that she'd sit still for that. But no point in arguing with a senior officer, especially one whose eyes were blazing now.

''Watch yourself, Douglas,'' he said. ''I want you to live long enough to graduate. After that, you'll become someone else's problem.''

Commander Korinthos walked away shaking his head, then looked for the other student who wouldn't divert. Several classmates clustered around to congratulate her.

''Good going, Allison,'' one said, his thumb up.

"I sure hope you weren't as shaky as I was on final," another admitted.

"Sweating all the way," she said, "but I wouldn't admit that to old Tiger Korinthos."

She'd been in trouble several times during flight training, never for want of knowledge or fortitude. Students weren't encouraged to test the outer limits of aircraft capability, or their own. She'd regularly done both.

Allison refilled her cup. Today's white-knuckles landing brought her one step closer to flying the F-14 Tomcat, the Navy's sleek, fearsome, world-class fighter. Once Washington changed its bureaucratic mind and allowed women as combat pilots, she thought, that would become possible. She'd read her first story about Amelia Earhart when she was seven years old.

The well-worn gold wings her father pinned on her at graduation a few weeks later were his own, earned as an enlisted aviation pilot more than thirty years before. He was one of a now-vanished breed of naval aviators drawn from the enlisted ranks of the service and designated "AP" for aviation pilot.

"These aren't very pretty, Allison," he'd said, "but maybe they'll bring you good luck, too."

Everyone else had to be satisfied with store-bought shiny new ones. Like Doug Douglas, those wings had flown all over the world. They, like he, had acquired dings and dents from hard years of service.

"I wouldn't trade them for a new Mercedes," she whispered, and kissed and hugged the lean, gray-haired man who had encouraged her ambition through the years that led to this moment. Designation as a naval aviator had been the happiest day of her life.

Less than a year later, Allison wondered if her relentless effort to succeed was worth it. The memorial service at the Naval Air Station Miramar outside San Diego was for an

F-14 fighter pilot, *her* fighter pilot. Lt. Michael Nelson's plane had plunged into the sea a week earlier during a training mission.

Bright young faces, lined older faces, and men who wore blue uniforms with gold lace stripes and gold wings on their breasts filled the chapel. Carefree, cocky exteriors carefully masked deeper feelings and inner struggles. Allison was the only woman aviator present. Michael had become the focus of her life.

Investigators struggled to learn what happened to Michael and his thirty-million-dollar F-14B Tomcat fighter. Searchers hadn't found enough of the aircraft to be sure. Nor had they found Michael. No distress call came in before he disappeared from the radar screen and "checked out of the net" forever.

When their relationship began, Allison had fought her instincts, logic, and Michael himself for two months. She hadn't joined the Navy to find a man. In fact, romance had no part in her plan at all. When she fell for the tall, easygoing Nebraskan who brought her flowers every Friday morning, her life changed course. The more she cared for Michael, the harder she tried to push him away with tough talk and near-insults. Now she regretted she hadn't expressed her love for him earlier.

Michael had pursued her with charm and resolve, refusing no for an answer when she rebuffed invitations, knocking on her door after she'd hung up on him. Allison had argued with him about something after their third, stormy date. She couldn't even remember the subject now.

"Now come here and listen to reason," he'd said, taking her hand and drawing her toward him.

"Reason! Why, you're a bullheaded fool," she said.

He'd silenced her with a firm, warm kiss, holding her head in his hands so she couldn't back away. Time to end that discussion anyway, she'd thought, not that he was ahead.

"Michael, stop that now—" was all she had time to say

before he again covered her mouth gently but firmly with his, cutting off her protest. He wrapped his arms around her, capturing her own between them. She felt as though she were beginning to melt.

Michael Nelson was the first man in her life who had successfully challenged her independent, determined nature. Several others had tried before that, but came away from the experience with bruised egos.

Today, here in the chapel, she remembered that night and afterward.

Her budding relationship with Michael continued for five months. He'd told her that he'd known long before she did that they were meant for each other.

"You need someone to keep you organized permanently," Michael had said one night when he left her off. His comment, predictably, started a battle.

Allison had railed on, until Michael took her in his arms and brought his lips within an inch of hers. She'd thought later that this young man who had broken horses to saddle as a boy had let her have her head only long enough to corral her.

"Now are you going to marry me or aren't you?" he'd whispered. "If you don't, you'll wander around and get into all sorts of trouble in this Navy. Besides, I love you."

They'd planned to become engaged before Christmas. Before that, he would take her home to meet his family in Nebraska. Then they'd fly to Norfolk where he'd ask her father for her hand the old-fashioned way.

Doug would have liked Michael, she thought. The retired command master chief knew the bright, confident young aviators who flew in the fighter and attack squadrons. He'd had more cockpit hours and more brushes with death than a squadron of them would have in a lifetime. Like most seasoned chiefs, Doug spotted phonies and four-flushers a block away.

Spartan, government-decor rooms on opposite ends of the bachelor officer quarters (or BOQ) at the naval air station were home for the young lovers. She'd felt increasingly alone each night when Nelson kissed her at the door of her room, ran his hand along her cheek, then walked down the passageway to his own. No one else asked Allison out anymore. They were known as a pair, and that made her happy.

Happily-ever-after had disappeared into the Pacific with Michael and his airplane. Together they'd planned a wedding, a honeymoon in Hawaii, flying for a few years, then children. She hadn't looked far enough ahead to decide whether she'd leave aviation when the kids came. They had talked only about raising their own generation of naval aviators.

To leave the Navy was something she would have considered only for him, not without pain. She'd have no reason, she thought, to think this way ever again. The Navy was once again her home, as it had been since she was a child.

The hardest part came at the end of the service in the station chapel. She had sung the refrain at countless services where her father's career took her as a child. The Navy Hymn, "Eternal Father, Strong to Save," was the prayer every sailor knew. Each Navy warfare specialty had its own verse. Some of the voices were older and subdued, others young and strong:

> "Lord, guard and guide the men who fly
> Through the great spaces in the sky
> Be with them traversing the air
> In darkling storms and sunlight fair
> Oh, hear us as we lift our prayer
> For those in peril in the air. Amen."

Civilians could cry in public. Naval aviators did not. Another silly male rule, Allison thought. She bit her tongue and glanced to the side at Michael's other colleagues.

She clenched her white gloves tightly in her left hand, gritted her teeth until her jaw hurt, and swallowed hard. As she looked down the row to her right, Adam's apples bobbed and men's faces tightened into masks. *It's always this way,* she thought. *This tradition, this stiff upper lip, this . . . infernal denial.*

Then, finally, the service was over. She walked quietly to the back of the chapel.

"I'm sorry, Allison," the first young flyer whispered as he took her hand in both of his, squeezing it gently. Others came by, one by one. Neither wife nor relative, she was entitled to none of the formal, official grief-support given by the Navy to families and spouses.

Saddest-looking of all was Petty Officer Tom Mitchell, Michael's plane captain, the enlisted man responsible for the F-14's maintenance checks.

"I don't know how to tell you how sorry I am, Ms. Douglas," Mitchell said.

"I know how you feel, Mitch. Believe me, I do." The bright young enlisted man looked like he badly needed someone to hug him, to tell him that the loss of Michael's aircraft wasn't his fault. She wasn't allowed to do that, either.

Still, she would not cry here. Only public tears were forbidden by the unwritten warriors' code. Anyone could go home and cry privately. Some, Allison thought, probably would.

Tonight, she knew, squadron pilots and flight officers would gather to toast Michael's memory. Some thought of the gathering as a kind of wake, she'd been told, a Viking funeral for a fallen warrior. Each knew that only a single mistake or faulty airplane part stood between them and him.

They hadn't invited her to join them tonight. Something primitively male dominated their meeting, mysteries they had to work out among themselves. Years from now, women aviators might attend. The men weren't ready yet.

When Allison closed her BOQ room door behind her,

emotion burst forth like a torrent from a broken dam. Bitter tears and racking sobs poured into her pillow until exhaustion mercifully silenced her hours later.

Before dawn, she rose to wash her swollen face in cold water. She owned no makeup to conceal shadows and puffiness. Lipstick and occasional eye shadow were all she ever used. Healthy, radiant skin was its own best makeup in the more normal times that had been her life up to now.

She must put Michael's death aside before it destroyed her. Distraction while flying was deadly. Never again would she become so close to someone who could be snatched from her. Never would she endure anything like this again, she thought . . . *never.*

Chapter Two

The evening after the memorial service, following dinner alone at the NAS Miramar officers club, Allison walked a long route back to the BOQ. She looked out along the flight line at sunset, where fighters sat silently in precise rows. The brazen sign in five-foot letters painted across the station's largest hangar announced to the world that this was "FIGHTERTOWN, USA."

Allison remembered the near-physical thrill the first time she'd landed here and seen that sign. Long before, she had decided to be part of the fighter community. Now, as she walked along in the growing darkness, she wasn't so sure.

She first knew she wanted to be a naval aviator when she stood on the ramp with her father at Naval Air Station Norfolk as a ten-year-old and watched F-4 Phantom fighters with Navy markings thunder commandingly into the evening sky. Their powerful, deafening roar dominated everything for miles around. The raw power and ferocious freedom of high-performance aircraft thrilled her. Only her father knew of her ambition then. Even he didn't believe she could ever realize it.

Even now, she was far from being a fighter pilot. The pressure was on to change old laws and regulations now that women's roles in the military services had expanded. But this one hadn't changed yet.

The fighter rides Allison had schemed herself into had fueled her determination. Superior flying ability and unflappable competence had placed her on the short list of applicants for flag pilot for the commander of the Pacific Fleet Naval Air Force. The three-star admiral with the short gray crew cut, who had himself flown regularly since before Allison was born, wanted to know who was up front when he flew around. He'd become qualified to fly more aircraft than anyone else in the Navy over the years, and he interviewed his own applicants.

"Lt. Douglas, what made you want this job? More important, why should I hire *you* as my flag pilot instead of someone with more hours in the T-39?"

"I'm the best T-39 driver on the West Coast, Admiral. I have VFR and IFR qualification and all the other tickets needed to fly the T-39 anywhere. I intend to be the best F-14 pilot in the fleet, so I need all the jet hours I can get. When Congress and the Navy stop prohibiting women aviators in combat squadrons, I want to be ready."

The admiral smiled, then chuckled as he seemed to remember an old story.

"You sound like another Douglas I flew with years ago," he said. "I was a young lieutenant in a composite squadron. He was an AP, an enlisted pilot flying R5D transports. A feisty guy, but one of the best. Brought home a couple of sick airplanes anyone else would have bailed out of. Tried to get him to work for me out in WESTPAC when he made master chief, but he wanted to stay in Norfolk because his daughter was in school. The girl wanted to become a naval aviator, he said."

"She did," Allison said softly. "She's the best T-39 pilot on the West Coast."

"Well then, I guess I better hire her before someone else does," the admiral said. "Prepare a flight plan for NAS Whidbey day after tomorrow. We launch at 0600. Lieutenant Commander Hobbs, my present pilot, will be leaving in two weeks. He'll ride along as copilot."

"Admiral, I'd be dishonest if I didn't say this is a pass-through job for me," Allison said. "T-39s are all right for now, but I won't spend my career as a flying bus driver."

"You've made that pretty clear, Ms. Douglas. I want a flag pilot who thinks like a fighter jock."

As Allison walked back to her car after the interview, she thought about the days long ago in Norfolk that the admiral had been speaking about.

Her mother had died suddenly during Allison's third year of high school, months after her father retired from the Navy. During his struggle to make the transition into a civilian job, he couldn't afford her college tuition. Few civilian jobs called for fiftyish master chiefs with thousands of prop pilot hours. Later, he'd landed a job with a charter service, flying small planes he called "bug smashers." The money still wasn't great.

She'd thought briefly about deferring college, but soon decided there was no time to waste. Allison didn't get an appointment to the Naval Academy, despite her high marks and aptitude. That would have meant a first-rate education and better assurance of flight school. Doug had said there was more than one way to get where she was going, and he helped her with alternatives.

Six years of part-time university courses while she worked full-time as a computer technician earned her a bachelor's degree in aeronautical engineering. She bartered part-time bookkeeping work for enough flying lessons to earn a private pilot's license. Doug went up with her after that and provided fine points not found in the book. Cessnas and Pipers were toys compared to the lightning-fast, powerful Navy warplanes. But they'd have to do for the time being.

Schooling had been a struggle, first to earn the money, then to master the advanced mathematics and science courses, and finally to deal with the faculty. Some professors didn't think aeronautical engineering was for women. She proved them wrong, placing third in her class. No time remained for social life, dates, or boyfriends.

* * *

When Allison walked into the Navy recruiting station before graduation, the chief petty officer in charge examined her qualifications. He shifted uneasily in his chair.

"Ms. Douglas, I don't mean to discourage you, but aviation programs have been slashed again by the latest budget cuts. A big chunk of flight school billets will go to Naval Academy graduates this year. Otherwise, only outstanding physical and mental candidates have a chance."

The officer procurement people she visited later that morning gave no encouragement.

"Your only snowball's chance in hell of getting into this program, Ms. Douglas, is if you're one very hard snowball," the aviator recruiter said.

"I am the hardest snowball you ever saw," she said calmly, "and I also have a rock inside." He chuckled at her plucky answer and handed over the mountain of application forms, but offered no encouragement. The next morning she returned the two pounds of completed paper to the recruiter. Neither of them smiled.

Her flight physical came a few days later.

"Ms. Douglas," the white-coated flight surgeon said, "I hope you're up to this. The bureau's granting no waivers these days, least of all on flight physicals."

"I'm not here to waste your time, Doctor." Her hazel eyes flashed at him. The fire in them belied the softness in her voice.

"A flight physical is tough," he said casually. "If you have any problems, we'll find them."

"Try me," she said. She'd waited too long to listen to this.

The physician saw firm, toned muscles, rosy skin, and clear eyes—the picture of an apparently very healthy female. A fine figure of a young woman, he thought. Too bad she was so intense.

"You women are lucky in one respect," the flight surgeon said. "Females have a lower physical fitness requirement for upper body strength. You have to do fewer push-ups and pull-ups.''

The hazel eyes burned now, her voice not nearly so soft this time.

"Doctor, no bureaucratic ninny in the Bureau of Naval Personnel will have any technicality, however slight, to weed me out of flight school. I'll test on the *male* requirements, thank you.'' Although she was smiling when the doctor looked up, the message in her voice was unmistakable.

"You sound like you're already in the Navy, Ms. Douglas,'' the doctor said.

"I was born in the Navy. Doug Douglas, the last force master chief at NAVAIRLANT, is my father.''

The flight surgeon nodded. He'd given the colorful, flinty force master chief several flight physicals. Douglas was the lean, salty character with bushy gray eyebrows who'd argued with admirals on behalf of the enlisted troops. Doug drew more water because he too wore the wings of a naval aviator. He'd logged more flying hours than most of the admirals, and they knew it.

"Will they call you Doug Douglas when you get out in the fleet?'' the doctor asked.

"There's only one Doug Douglas,'' she said. "They'll have to call me something else.''

"You sound like a chip off the old block,'' the doctor said.

From then on, she'd be "Chip'' Douglas.

Allison exceeded the required pull-ups and push-ups for males, halved the required time for the run, and finished in the ninetieth percentile for male physical fitness testing. Months of boring workouts and arduous runs in the damp, predawn Tidewater darkness before work and school had paid off.

Two F-14s screamed down the near-dark Miramar runway, their running lights twinkling, as Allison continued her walk back to the BOQ. The physical, she thought, had been easy compared to what followed a few days later.

The officer selection board convened to interview applicants at the Norfolk Naval Air Station included three aviators among its five members. The senior member was a captain from the staff of the Commander, Naval Air Force, Atlantic Fleet. When she walked into the interview room, the faces around the table with the long green tablecloth showed no emotion and even less encouragement.

They were here to weed her out, she thought.

During the past four years she'd analyzed every question such a board could ask, forming an answer to each one. She might miss one or two, she thought, but not many.

The gray-haired aviation captain, who looked least convinced of all, leaned forward. He engaged her eyes as he spoke.

"Naval aviation is an unconventional job, for a man or a woman. Why do you want to be a naval aviator, Ms. Douglas?"

"It runs in my family, Captain."

"Was your father an aviator?"

"Yes." She wanted to say more, but it would wait.

The captain leaned forward as he spoke.

"What did he fly, Ms. Douglas?"

"The enlisted aviation pilots flew only transports, Captain. My father logged more hours in the R5D and the C-130 than any other pilot in the Atlantic Fleet."

The captain's expression told her he now knew which Douglas was her father.

"Did you take the degree in aeronautical engineering with this in mind?"

She shrugged casually, broke her direct eye contact with him for a second or two, then locked back on.

"I could think of no better preparation." She knew that few except Naval Academy graduates came to the service with such credentials.

"Have you ever flown in a single-engine aircraft, Ms.

Douglas—a light plane? Flying in smaller aircraft is different than riding in airliners.''

"Somewhere in that pile of paper is a copy of my private pilot's license, Captain. I have logged additional hours toward a commercial ticket.''

The questions continued for almost an hour. The average candidate received fifteen minutes. A dozen male applicants milled about uneasily outside the room.

Inside the oak-paneled doors, the questions became tougher. Her quick, assured answers continued. Board members sought the elusive question that would stump her.

Allison felt the clammy coolness of stress perspiration. She'd prepared for this, she thought, for longer than the younger board members had been in the Navy.

"What type of aircraft do you want to fly—fixed-wing or helicopters?'' the captain asked, winding down toward the end with a seemingly innocent question.

"Fighters, Captain, I want to fly fighters. F-14s preferably, A-6s or F-18s otherwise. T-39s, S-3s, C-2s or anything else with a tailhook will do in the meantime.''

The other aviators on the board leaned forward. The woman knew the Navy's aircraft inventory well, and also knew exactly what she wanted. When the four-striper looked up, it was into the full force of Allison's unwavering hazel stare.

"One final question, Ms. Douglas,'' the captain said. At last this ordeal would end. He leaned forward before he spoke. "Flight school is tough to get into, very tough. We'll interview ten, maybe fifteen, fully qualified applicants for each one who goes to Pensacola. I won't send anyone there who I think will wash out. How badly do you want to be a naval aviator, Ms. Douglas?''

The answer shot back immediately.

"I want it badly enough to go to college six years at night for a degree, to get a pilot's license in my off hours while holding down a full-time job. I've finished everything I've started in my life thus far, and I *will* finish flight school too. And when I finish that, Captain, I *will* fly the Navy's fighters.'' Her gaze never wavered.

"Thank you, Ms. Douglas, that will be all.''

As she walked past the roomful of other applicants, out into the morning sunshine, Allison knew her fate was being settled by the men around the table with the long green cloth. A downcheck here would be a major setback.

After she closed the large, oak-paneled door behind her, the aviation captain spoke to the four other men in the room.

"Okay, boys, what do you think of Ms. Douglas?'' he said as he pulled together the papers from her file.

When he looked up, four right thumbs were pointed toward the ceiling.

Six weeks later, an envelope from the bureau sat on top of the pile of mail she pulled from the mailbox when she arrived home from work. Allison squealed with delight as she read it, dancing around the kitchen in unrestrained glee. She couldn't wait for her father to come home an hour later.

The chief of naval personnel, the letter said, was pleased to inform her that she had been selected to attend flight training, after successful completion of the aviation officer candidate course.

She'd heard that AOCS, the school leading to an ensign's commission before flight school, was a bearish sixteen-week ordeal. Weak sisters, male and female, were culled out during this process. High-pressure physical and mental stress provided by omnipresent Marine drill instructors and tough technical academics were the crucible. Half a century ago, the Navy had learned that washing out nonstarters was cheaper here than during the expensive flight training program after commissioning.

"Guess what?'' she said as Doug walked in the door, her face a glum mask. She held up the letter from the bureau. Her father knew the odds against success and had been prepared to console her.

"That's okay, Allison, you can reapply. Build up some more flying hours and try again," he said as he came across the room to hug her.

"The next flying this kid does will be in a *Navy* airplane," she said, her expression changed now to a broad smile.

Doug Douglas walked into his bedroom and removed the aviator wings from the suit of dress blues he planned to be buried in. He put the scratched, worn gold insignia on the kitchen table.

"These are yours, when you earn them," he said. She hugged the old man as tears ran down her cheeks.

During many dark nights preceding crucial tests in the months that followed, she recalled those wings. The aviation class inexorably shrank in size as relentless pressure whittled away at the group. If the old man could earn wings, she reminded herself, she wasn't his daughter if *she* could not.

He had gone to the recruiting station to watch her raise her hand. Doug knew the oath of enlistment by heart. Allison knew it too, the recruiting officer soon learned. She ignored the copy of the enlistment contract she'd been given to read from.

"I, Allison Douglas," she said, "do solemnly swear that I will support and defend the Constitution of the United States against all enemies, foreign and domestic; that I will bear truth, faith and allegiance to the same; and that I will obey the orders of the President of the United States and the orders of the officers appointed over me, according to regulations and the Uniform Code of Military Justice. So help me God."

"Welcome to the United States Navy," the recruiting officer had said as he felt her strong, confident handshake.

Now, she thought as Miramar's BOQ loomed ahead of her in the growing darkness, that seemed a very long time ago.

Chapter Three

The two months had passed quickly since Michael's death, Allison thought as she stretched out after a hard run and a shower. She'd volunteered for extra flights, took holiday duties for married friends, did special squadron projects, and baby-sat the children for her enlisted crew chief. Anything to keep from thinking too much.

The spark that made her so vibrant while Michael lived was snuffed out. She hardly thought of herself as a woman anymore. Her appearance was "regulation"—hair properly trimmed, uniforms sharply pressed. Seldom did she wear anything frilly now during off-duty hours. There was no one to dress up for.

Allison ran for an hour each evening, returning breathless and perspiring, ready for sleep. She tried hard to forget the memories of Michael, but they wouldn't go away.

Several young aviators had invaded her self-imposed isolation with invitations to dinner, concerts, and other dates. Some tried to ease her pain; others appeared genuinely taken with her. None of them interested her now.

"Listen, Allison," one of Michael's friends had said after several turndowns, "he wouldn't want you to do this to yourself. He'd want you to be happy. Remember your good times with him, but move on and live. Regardless of whom you decide to go out with, think about going out with *someone*."

No one like Michael would ever come along again, she thought. Like no other man she'd ever met, he had brought her love and the promise of a special future together. Then he was snatched away forever. For now, she drifted, alone.

Sleep came easily after the hard run.

Her vivid dream re-created the picnic with Michael at an isolated beach far up the coast, north of San Diego. After two months of dinner-and-talk dates, the zoo, Mission Valley, and Old Town, Michael decided on something more daring. He'd parked the car out of sight beside the coastal highway and led her down a steep, rocky incline. It was a good thing Michael held the picnic basket. A mountain goat would balk at this narrow, pebble-strewn dirt path, she'd thought.

As she climbed cautiously down the rocky hillside, she knew that being alone together in this isolated place would test her confidence in him. Perhaps, she thought, her agreement to come here sent the wrong message. At the same time, many women friends, in and out of the Navy, chided her for her old-fashioned views. They said she'd end up an old maid. Others, she recalled, had told her she would never become a naval aviator. As persistent in her beliefs as she was about her career, Allison still believed that some things must wait for marriage.

The small patch of beach carved out between two rock formations reached toward the surf. Other rocks further back created a smaller, more intimate shield from the sea. Pine trees and heavy brush hid the cove from the road. Allison changed into her bathing suit among the sheltered rocks. It was their own private preserve, she'd thought, hidden from the world. Perhaps too hidden, too isolated. She might have been foolish to do this.

As she looked around the horizon and up the steep incline, the world seemed far away. They weren't Navy pilots today, simply young people discovering each other. The few boats she saw were miles away near the horizon.

They frolicked in the crashing surf like carefree children. She playfully dashed salt water in great handfuls into his face, making his eyes sting. He dove under and grabbed her legs, trying to bring her down, as she swung and splashed at him.

Then they found excuses to draw each other closer. Salty surf broke over them, pushing her toward him. Her arms held him as their mouths and eyes filled with seawater. Finally they stood in the gently eddying water between waves, arms around each other, the waters between them, and kissed gently.

"I must look like a drowned rat," she'd gasped.

"You're beautiful, Allison," he whispered into her ear, sounding more serious, and more urgent, than she expected.

Michael kissed her, took her hand wordlessly, and walked with her up the beach. Just as well, she thought. It was time to cool off and dry off.

He opened the picnic basket and laid out chicken, salad, and cold drinks on a large blanket in the sand. She'd known for weeks that she was in love with him. At first, she'd denied it. After endless struggle toward an aviation career, Allison now suspected that being a fighter pilot might not be life's ultimate achievement after all.

Hazy sun, warm sand, the swimming, and a leisurely lunch had created a mellow, magical mood. Whispering breezes and pounding surf alternated in the background as a portable CD played light, romantic music.

As she lazed on the blanket over the yielding sand, her consciousness drifted until she felt his first gentle kiss. A warm feeling coursed through her. The pervasive thrill returned each time she had been with him. She sighed.

Allison had fought involvement for years, avoiding commitment to anything but her career. Each time she returned home from being with Michael and closed her door, though, she felt incomplete, strange, in conflict. Perhaps she'd fought too long. She would let today take its course.

"Michael, it's beautiful here," she said, opening her eyes. She needed to catch her breath for a moment.

"Hmm," he replied, "and so are you." He kissed her again.

"Do you bring all the girls here?"

"Only dark-haired women flag pilots for COMNAV-AIRPAC."

Allison knew it was time to stop talking. Michael kissed her again. A light breeze replaced the warmth of the sun as clouds scudded across it.

She hoped he didn't notice her trembling. She wasn't the self-confident Allison Douglas of yesterday, or even this morning, she thought.

Once again she listened to the soft breaking of the waves on the beach as she closed her eyes.

The next thing she remembered was his fingers gently touching her face. His lips, close to her ear, said "I love you, Allison." So that was why he'd brought her here—to tell her this, and whatever else went with it.

The sun was dipping toward the horizon over the sea. Time to go home. But not yet, she thought. As the shadows lengthened, she pushed him gently down on the blanket and kissed him as fervently as he had her. She hadn't said she loved him then, but tried to tell him without words.

Her languorous dream now ended abruptly. The raucous, abrasive sound of the alarm clock demanded her immediate attention. She awoke, not rested and warm as she'd hoped, but clammy and shaken. Allison thought time would help her recover, regain her perspective and her strength, and put Michael's death behind her. She'd been wrong. Never had she felt more helpless or alone. Never again would she let this happen, she thought—never again.

Chapter Four

Allison became nervous after she arrived at Miramar's T-39 hangar on Tuesday morning. A message summoned her to see the naval air force chief of staff at the air station on North Island, across the Coronado Bridge. She wondered what was wrong. The old boy never issued social invitations.

"Come in, Chip. Want some coffee?" Once the captain offered hospitality, she relaxed.

"No thank you, sir. What's up?"

"The admiral's being transferred to Washington," he said. "The official announcement will break in a few days, but he wants the personal staff to know first. The incoming boss has his own flag pilot. Our leader wants to ensure you have a set of orders that will help your career. Tell me what you'd like and I'll try to land it for you."

"Same as ever. Fighters. I want to fly fleet fighters, sir. Whatever brings me closer to that is what I want."

He frowned. She knew no operational fighter jobs existed for women. The captain leaned back in the chair, silent for a moment.

"To do that, whenever it happens, you must keep flying, a job which allows you more jet flight hours, one that looks good to a selection board. When Washington allows women in combat squadrons, they'll pick the most experienced jet jockeys. You must keep flying and broaden your experience."

"What about test pilot school?" she said, only half-joking.

"That's about the only way a woman gets to fly a fighter in today's Navy, but it's too early in your career. Those school seats are all done by a Washington selection board. It's a tough engineering curriculum. You have the right idea, though," he said. "Your superb flying record and that aeronautical engineering degree will work for you. TPS will take time, but it's a live possibility. I'll do whatever I can."

A transfer away might be better, she thought as she weaved through mid-morning traffic across the Coronado Bridge and up the interstate to Miramar. Leaving would mitigate the painful daily reminders of Michael. Working around fighters you couldn't fly, she thought, was like being thirsty near a fountain where you couldn't drink.

As she drove through the base on her way back to the hangar, she heard the roar of an F-14 taking off. The silver airplane rocketed skyward, turning toward the Pacific.

She'd cajoled F-14 rides from Michael and others, and she itched to put a first-line fighter through its paces. The powerful, agile fighter flew faster straight up than her own aircraft in level flight at full throttle.

She telephoned her father when the orders arrived two weeks later.

"Dad, it's a baby-sitting job. Jet training instructor for student aviators at Meridian. I couldn't be further away from fighters," she said. She'd learned to fly jet trainers at the big base before she earned her wings.

"Sure, and I'd rather drive a BMW than my old Chevy," he replied. "Quit your bellyaching. You're flying. You'll log plenty of jet time, do lots of cross-country hops. With the budget cuts, any cockpit job these days is gravy. You're lucky some chauvinist turkey in BUPERS aviation assignments didn't shuffle you off to a desk somewhere to open a flying job for one of his buddies."

She hadn't thought about that. Only the admiral's personal intervention had kept her in flying status. The assignment detailers knew better than to buck a powerful three-star. Allison suspected she had much to learn about Navy politics.

"You're right, Dad. I should be more grateful."

"You're darn right, you should. Listen, Allison, those instructors at Meridian are handpicked fleet-seaters coming ashore after three to five years on carriers. They'll teach you a lot, if you listen. Each one has more carrier traps than you have runway landings. Did the old man at AIR-PAC take care of you on your fitness report?"

"Straight bullets, recommendation for early promotion, and—"

"Hey, that's all right!" her father broke in. No better fitness report existed. "What else were you going to say?" Doug chortled with pride.

"Test pilot school. The admiral recommended me for test pilot school." Silence at the other end of the line.

"Dad, did you hear that?"

"Life doesn't get any better than that as a 'jg'. The old man must really like you."

"I flew him all over the country this past year—got him home once after an engine failed at twenty thousand feet and another time after lightning struck. Never so much as blew a tire while I worked for him. The admiral had no reason to complain."

"You're being modest," Doug said. "Those fusty old-time flag officers don't give away anything to female pilots. Look, you've got more ahead than flying transports for the rest of your career. No telling what will happen in the next couple of years. Right now you've got the world by the ear, so make the most of it."

"I should spend more time looking at the bright side," she said.

"You bet you should. Hey, I almost forgot. A shipmate of mine from Norfolk, a senior chief yeoman named Cora Wade-Cochrane, had orders to Meridian a while back. Cora and your mother were great friends. She still sends a Christmas card each year. The woman has more savvy than a barrel of commanders. Her husband was a chief machinist's mate who died in a shipboard engineering accident. She hasn't remarried, far as I know.''

The comment reminded Allison that her father was alone too. ''I'll look her up when I get there,'' she said. ''Meanwhile, take care of yourself, Dad. You've kept my perspective squared away.''

Meridian would be okay after all, she thought. Any cockpit, even a jet trainer with a shaky student aviator up front, was better than the fanciest desk in the Navy.

Chapter Five

Allison's two-thousand-mile drive along I-10 through the western desert to El Paso, across Texas and Louisiana, up I-55 to Jackson, and east to Meridian, Mississippi, provided time to think.

Her mind told her time and again that Michael wouldn't want her to grieve for him. He'd always done his best without regrets, never looked back. Some things about him she would never forget. Other hard lessons she vowed never to relearn.

She remembered Meridian's sprawling air station. A master jet training base in east central Mississippi with three ten-thousand-foot runways, it ran at a slower pace than Miramar's dynamic, fleet-oriented Fightertown.

The sharp salute from a white-gloved woman sentry at the station gate seemed a good omen.

"Where does Training Squadron Six call home these days?" she asked the woman as she pulled up in her four-year-old Chevy.

"TRARON SIX? Okay, Lieutenant, follow the signs for Air Training Wing One. They're down in that same area. Can't miss it. Here's a station map for you that should help."

Perhaps there was more room for women now in the flight training side of naval aviation. She'd had to fight for her place, make her own reputation for competence among the males at Miramar. She would do that again here if necessary, she thought.

After leaving her orders and records at the squadron headquarters, Allison checked into the bachelor officer quarters. A sunny, warm day to report aboard was another good sign.

She wrestled a bulky aviator's bag partway up the stairs in one hand as she held a large civilian suitcase in the other.

"Can I bear a hand with that?" a voice said from behind her.

When she turned, a tall, red-haired lieutenant in a sharply pressed tropical white uniform smiled up at her. Gold aviator wings straddled ribbons which, at a glance, revealed he had flown in combat during the Gulf War. His handsome, clean-cut features, open smile, and fit, resilient body classified him as a hunk by any measure, she thought.

"Yes, thanks. This gear wasn't made for narrow ladders."

"I think we can fix that," he said as he took the larger of the two bags from her.

His blue eyes, which had locked on hers like a radar, flitted for an instant to her uniform blouse. Checking for aviator wings, she thought.

"Passing through, or here for duty?" he asked lightly as they continued up the stairs.

"Duty. TRARON SIX as a flight instructor." Less than three years ago, she had been a student herself. That seemed a lifetime ago.

"Welcome aboard. I'm Rusty O'Hara. We'll be flying together. I'm also in SIX."

"Chip Douglas," she said, extending her free hand now that they'd reached the top of the stairs.

"Where did you get that handle?" he said.

She laughed. "My father was an aviator and I'm a chip off the old block. Civilians call me Allison."

"Some people like Jeff better than Rusty, too. I like Allison."

"I've been called worse," she said. She quickly perceived the unflattering range of possible meanings and bit her tongue. An awkward first impression, she thought.

"Haven't we all?" O'Hara responded. "I'm off this afternoon. Had the squadron duty last night. If you'd like, I'll give you a refresher tour of the base. They've moved some things around in the last couple of years."

O'Hara returned a half-hour later with a "Welcome Aboard" package of material about the base and the surrounding area.

"Read all this carefully," O'Hara said with mock seriousness as he handed her the envelope. "There will be a one-hundred question quiz tomorrow at 0900."

His homework assignment sounded like the days in aviation officer candidate school. They both laughed. Her first good laugh with a man since Michael died felt liberating.

"We do squadron 'hail and farewells' on Fridays after classes are over. We introduce new folks, laugh, and scratch over a drink or two, then swap stories about the strange antics of the students. You'll get an earful and meet all the instructors."

"Already on my knee pad," she said, referring to the aviator's clipboard for scrawling information while flying.

They rode around the base in his Toyota, then stopped at the cafeteria for lunch and drove for an hour until she knew again where everything was located.

"Thanks, Rusty, the tour helped a lot. They *did* move a bunch of things without consulting me," she said, shaking his hand when he dropped her off at the BOQ.

"Okay, Chip. See you at the squadron tomorrow . . . and Friday afternoon at the officer's club.

"Count on it," she said, gesturing with her thumb up. The new assignment already looked promising. She wondered as she walked up the stairs how this handsome, engaging man had acquired all those personal decorations.

After the tour, O'Hara walked to his own room at the other end of the BOQ. He'd wanted to ask the beautiful young aviator with the hazel eyes to dinner. Instinct told him to fly low and slow. He'd seized the first opportunity to impress her; perhaps he could get to know her better as time went on. He wouldn't mind foreclosing the inevitable competition in advance, but knew that wouldn't work. A woman handpicked to teach aviation among a bunch of fighter and attack pilots was independent enough to make up her own mind.

Allison riffled through the dog-eared, scribbled-in station phone directory in her BOQ room and found Senior Chief Yeoman Cora Wade-Cochrane. Her father hadn't told her that his old shipmate was now the commodore's writer at the station, but that didn't surprise her. Dad knew everyone. She dialed the office and introduced herself.

"Things are slow today," Cora's soft voice said. "The commodore's out of town. Come on over and have some coffee."

Perhaps Cora's prematurely gray hair made her look motherly, Allison thought when they met. They spoke for almost an hour about the base and how things really ran. Beneath Cora's softness Allison detected a strong, determined core. She remembered what her father had said about Cora being widowed. Allison understood part of what that meant.

"Your father's a good man," Cora said. "A straight shooter in a world full of black hats. I was very sad about your mother."

They talked about her father, and Allison's ambition to fly fighters.

"That's only a matter of time," Cora said. "From what I can see, it won't be much longer. Women have come a long way in a few years, mostly because we've proven ourselves at every turn."

"I hope you're right, Cora. Right now the prospects don't look great," Allison replied.

"Because you're Doug's daughter, I won't hold being an officer against you," Cora said, smiling.

Allison had been a chief petty officer's daughter long enough to know what she meant. When she walked out into the warmth of the afternoon Mississippi sun, Allison knew life would be better here. She'd call her father tonight to assure him she had arrived safely.

Tired from long days of driving, she wanted to "crash and burn" after an early dinner. She hoped that dreamless sleep would replace her restlessness since Michael's death. She'd found a new place, a new start.

She thought again of Rusty O'Hara. At first glance, the ranking decoration on the young lieutenant's uniform looked like a Distinguished Flying Cross, the nation's highest combat aviation award. When she'd looked again later, she knew she was right.

Chapter Six

Friday afternoons at the NAS Meridian Officers' Club would likely be typical of the TGIF celebrations she'd come to expect, Allison thought. Before Michael ran off the rest of the herd at Miramar, she'd dealt single-handedly with frisky single pilots. While a training command would have more married officers, she expected some bachelors to react.

Two years earlier, fellow students at Pensacola had tried predictable, daring runs. Each male aviator, she'd learned, thought he was God's gift to women. But then, they were expected to be confident and aggressive by nature. Once a woman was linked steadily to one of them, the others generally broke off. Until that happened, any attractive woman was a fair target.

Rusty arrived early, freshly showered and in a new uniform. Instinct told him Allison knew her own mind and couldn't be moved on at any pace faster than she wanted. He loitered near the lounge entrance to spot her coming through the door. When she did, several other squadron people were with her.

"Hi, Chip," he said, trying to be casual. "Get you a welcome drink?"

"Thanks, Rusty," she responded with a smile. "That's kind of you. White wine spritzer, please."

* * *

He'd been waiting, she thought, but that was nice—flattering, actually. He was bright, thoughtful, seemed a straight shooter, and had earned a DFC. He brought her the wine and stayed to chat.

"Best Friday turnout we've had in months," he said. "I've never seen more wives here. Maybe the word's out that we have fun here. Or perhaps they've heard we get a little out of control, and want to calm down the rumpus room."

Or maybe, Allison thought, the word's around about the new female instructor. This had happened to her before, at Miramar. Some wives, she'd learned, regarded a single woman aviator who worked near their husbands as a threat. But they usually liked and admired Allison after they met her, and became friendly.

After mingling for a while, Allison prompted an officer who'd been in Rusty's squadron during the Gulf War to describe O'Hara's combat record.

"Old Rusty jumped those Iraqi fighters so fast and got so close that he made their pilots itch. Not for long, though. He's the only one around who could darn near run heat-seeking missiles up a MIG tailpipe with visual bearings. That became his trademark. We think he was one reason some of their pilots defected to Iran and the rest stayed on the ground. Depending on who you talk to, Rusty should either teach aerial tactics at 'Top Gun,' or have his head candled."

The story made her think of Michael, who'd also lived to take chances. Perhaps Michael had taken one too many that sunny morning over the Pacific.

In the ladies' room, Allison overheard two wives who had come in to refresh their makeup.

"What do you think of the new woman instructor?" one said.

"Good-looking. Smart. She can have anyone or anything

she wants if she plays it right. I'll have to keep George on a short leash.''

"Maybe she's looking for a husband.''

"That's okay . . . as long as it's not mine,'' the other woman said, and both laughed. "I don't think we need to worry. Someone with her brains and looks could've had a husband years ago if she wanted to. That gal didn't come here to find one.''

"As long as she keeps her hands off what doesn't belong to her, I don't care.''

Within an hour, Allison had met every squadron officer, and most wives, at the Friday afternoon ritual. The group seemed generally friendly, and she was beginning to feel at home.

Rusty watched Allison make her way around the room. He waited until the crowd thinned out before he approached her again. Lt. Theodore "Slick" Chadwick appeared to be making a run, Rusty noticed. He sauntered over to where Chadwick had engaged Allison in conversation. Rusty's drive around the base with Allison had revealed her affection for Mexican food. She'd told him of several favorite restaurants, including Mexican Village, known to aviators as MEXPAC, on Coronado.

"Tonight would be a good time to run a road reconnaissance on that Mexican place I told you about downtown, Chip, if you're ready to tackle some refried beans and jalapeños,'' Rusty said.

"I was about to ask Allison if she wanted to try a steak at Weidman's,'' Chadwick parried. "They have a very continental wine list,'' he added.

Chadwick's one-upmanship was instant and sure, she thought. Perhaps that explained his nickname.

"Thank you both. Your hospitality is overwhelming,'' she said, "but it's been a busy first week. I'm overdue to catch up on essentials tonight. Perhaps another time.''

*   *   *

Cora Cochrane's chat the day she'd arrived had been informative. Allison learned that Ted Chadwick was the scion of an old Navy family, a Naval Academy graduate. His father, a three-star vice admiral in Washington, dealt often with the air training wing commodore. Admiral Chadwick would likely have a career-enhancing senior staff job in Washington waiting two years from now when Ted completed his requisite ticket-punch of training students.

Since he'd arrived at TRARON SIX, Cora said, Chadwick had scheduled so many cross-country student training flights to Washington's Andrews Air Force Base that he no longer needed a navigation chart. Ted must have close family ties, Allison concluded. Why else fly north so often?

Rusty intercepted her as she left the club.

"If you've whipped those essentials by tomorrow night," he said, "we can take on Mama Rosita's. I guarantee this place won't let you nod off. And the chilies, those wonderful chilies . . ." O'Hara kissed his fingertips.

"You've talked me into it," she said, and rested her hand lightly on his arm.

Cora said Rusty had come into naval aviation the hard way. Like herself, Allison thought. With no influential contacts or family help, he'd made his mark by performance. His boyish charm belied the toughness that had earned him the Distinguished Flying Cross and a half-dozen Air Medals. Many aviators had been awarded such decorations for daring posthumously. That thought disturbed her.

The following evening, they immersed themselves in the raucous, crowded Mexican cantina, where the food was spicy, taped mariachi music blared, and casually dressed customers reveled in a carefree atmosphere. Not a fancy place, but relaxed and fun, she thought. Her good humor and enthusiasm were returning. Accepting Rusty's invitation had been a good idea.

"What did you do before you came here?" she asked him while they munched on chips and salsa as they waited for the main course. She also wanted his account of the story.

"I flew in the Persian Gulf during the unpleasantness over there," he replied. "We'd play chicken with Iraqi MIGs until they didn't like the game anymore. The losers in that drill bailed out, if they were lucky. A character-building experience . . . for them." No mention of his personal awards. She liked his self-effacing response.

When he took her home, Rusty kissed her lightly on the cheek, moving close enough that she could smell the manly scent of him. As he held her lightly, his hands were strong but gentle.

Later, in her room, as Allison stretched out on the bed, her thoughts stayed with Rusty. He was an attractive man who was in a fine position to get himself killed. Not that he'd do it here. The Naval Air Training Command was strict about careful flying while instructing students. Even given the strange things student aviators sometimes did, the command safety record was superb.

Rusty's luck might not fail until he returned to the fleet, during an exercise, or at a fighter-school refresher, where he would cut some intricate maneuver too fine, to preserve his reputation. On the other hand, he'd survived Gulf War combat. Perhaps it was luck, she thought, or more likely, he was more skilled than his competition.

Only if she stopped now could she avoid repeating what happened with Michael. Tonight had reawakened her interest in attractive males, and Rusty in particular. The companionship of a charming man made her feel alive again.

She felt ready for a strong man's arms around her, the right man. Michael had shown her she was meant to be loved, and to love. He'd opened up a new chapter in her life.

But Michael wasn't ever coming back. No life worth living was without risk, Allison thought as she drifted off to sleep. Now it was time to live again.

The following morning, the BOQ desk clerk handed her

a message slip from Ted Chadwick. The phone call had come in the previous night while she was out with Rusty.

Steaks sighted up ahead, the message read. *Let's roll in and wipe 'em out Sunday night if you're free.* There was a phone number. The carefully worded message said nothing romantic.

She walked back to her room, considering the invitation. No sense spending the evening alone in a command full of attractive, single men. No reason to be pinned down only to Rusty O'Hara, either. She wondered why Ted hadn't asked her for Saturday night, instead of the usually quiet Sunday. No matter, she thought as she dialed Ted's number.

Chapter Seven

Nice car, Allison thought as she walked toward the BOQ parking lot. Ted Chadwick's red BMW convertible, parked outside when he came to pick her up, gleamed in the late-afternoon sunlight. His Beemer was the only one she knew of in the squadron.

Ted's clothes, although casual, were well tailored and, she guessed, expensive. A healthy tan and lean, muscled body confirmed regular outdoor exercise. His clean-cut face, strong chin, and black hair augmented his intelligent conversation at the officers' club. His polished style contrasted with Rusty's laid-back Midwestern manner.

Perhaps she should trade in the old Chevy and drive a sports car if she expected to be a fighter pilot, Allison thought whimsically. Raised in a family where money was often short, wheels were transportation. A car as a social statement was foreign to her.

"Ready for a side of beef or some portion thereof?" Ted asked.

Allison's stylish, relaxed long-sleeved blouse and comfortable slacks accentuated her attractiveness without over-emphasizing her figure. The tailored Navy uniform did that better. Her outfit was sleek without being fussy.

"I can handle a prime rib, and perhaps the salad bar," she bantered as they walked to his car.

While Ted drove the twenty miles into town across the Mississippi countryside, Allison tossed her hair in the breeze, enjoying easy conversation and the taped elegance of Handel's *Music for the Royal Fireworks* on the BMW's stereo. Classical music was another favorite she'd begun to spend more time with.

Ted liked to talk. He appeared confident and in control of his future, she thought. Not one to shoot from the hip. His comments about local and national events were as sensitive to political currents as he'd be to air currents while flying. He'd probably succeed on a senior Washington staff, where promising officers set their course for the future. This man, she thought, would be less inclined to kill himself recklessly in an airplane, and more likely to live to reach senior rank and high command.

"What's on your dream sheet for your next assignment?" Ted asked, bringing her back from her reverie.

"A fleet fighter squadron," she replied, "after the RAG, of course." The Replacement Air Group trained fleet pilots to qualify in carrier aircraft.

"A tall ambition," he said as he looked at her, his hair blowing in the breeze. "Have you convinced the Secretary of Defense to change the policy on women yet?"

"He hasn't returned my phone calls, but there are enough of us out here now. Our track record proves we can hack it. We'll get his attention, or somebody's, soon. Despite what the old boy network thinks, flying fighters doesn't require testosterone."

"What's your airplane of choice?"

"The F-14. I want to be one of the first female Tomcats."

"Settle for an F-18 if you had to?"

"Life's full of compromises," she said. "But why fly a Chevy if you can fly a Cadillac?" Allison thought of her own aged Chevy. She probably could afford something more upscale. Ted's glitzy BMW *was* more appealing.

"You're a real hired killer, Allison," he chuckled.

"I'd rather terrify the bad guys into submission—what they call deterrence, isn't it? If they can't take the hint, the outcome becomes their problem." She shrugged.

Allison was not yet comfortable with Ted's sophisticated style, although time might fix that. Dealing with him would be a learning opportunity, she decided.

Ted's interactions with others tended to draw people out, while he kept his thoughts to himself. Interesting but different, Allison mused.

Rusty disliked Ted, she thought. He'd said nothing, but their brief exchange at the club revealed that, subtly but surely.

Rusty preferred jeans and an old shirt for outings to Mexican restaurants, and she knew from their conversation that he liked to walk in country fields or fish in remote creeks. She liked his carefree banter about things they had in common.

But she was here now with Ted. Cora had told her that Weidman's, one of the town's oldest restaurants, was famous for prime beef, civilized atmosphere, and Meridian's best wine list.

"What's your pleasure?" Ted asked, handing her the wine list. They'd already selected prime rib for the main course. Allison reviewed the card, then handed it back to him. She felt he was testing her knowledge.

"Not a bad one in the bunch," she said, certain that was true because this was Weidman's. "Any red you choose will be fine, Ted. I'm not much of a drinker."

He picked a vintage cabernet sauvignon.

"You were right," she said after she sipped the smooth cabernet and cut into the tender prime rib. "This place is delightful."

"Life's too short not to enjoy the best of everything," he said as he toasted her.

From holding her chair at the table to the selection of a vintage wine, she'd never been more catered to in her life. Ted listened well and always said and did the right thing, she thought. But then, she'd been out with few men. *If only he knew how inexperienced I am.*

The bill at Weidman's was four times what Rusty had

spent at the Mexican place. Ted covered it routinely with a well-worn gold credit card. Perhaps Ted's choice of restaurants was part of his message.

The exquisite social graces that Ted cultivated had never interested her before. That might mark the difference between an admiral's son and a chief petty officer's daughter. He might be quite a catch, or all manners and no substance. Who knows? she thought. For now, she wanted light, casual relationships. One day, she might have to choose between him and Rusty, or perhaps others. For now, she'd enjoy window-shopping.

"Where will *you* go from here, Ted?" Allison had watched him, seemingly deep in thought, for a few minutes as they drove along listening to the mesmerizing music of Mozart.

"Probably one of the Washington staffs, the obligatory D.C. shore-duty checkoff," he said. He made it sound unimportant. "After that, another squadron at sea."

The squadron tour which followed at that point in his career, she thought, would be critically important to steer him toward early command.

"There are some great apartments near where I live," he said as they passed his neighborhood on the way back to the base. "Some good ones will come open soon. I know the property manager. She'll show them to you, if you like." No harm looking, Allison thought.

When Ted drove into the BOQ parking lot the place was lit only with dim streetlights.

"What a great evening you've made it, Allison," he said, taking her hand in his when they arrived at the door of her room.

"I enjoyed it very much," she replied. A pang went through her as she thought of another BOQ, half a continent away, and similar times with Michael. She waited for Ted to kiss her.

"Let's do this again soon," he said. He squeezed her hand and brushed his lips lightly across her cheek.

When she closed the door, Allison felt confused. She'd expected him to come on stronger.

As he drove away from the BOQ and down the darkened road, Ted was confident his charm had worked. She'd listened attentively. Allison was unsophisticated, he thought. A chief's daughter wouldn't have exquisite social graces, although this one was intelligent and quick.

Her hazel eyes hid a smoldering fire; her firm figure showed vibrant femininity. She appeared oblivious to her own intelligence and charm. The woman had courage to invade a male preserve full of risk, combat, and high technology. That alone made her worthy of study. He'd never pursued a woman aviator before. Allison would be a challenge.

His competition was obvious. O'Hara had arrived at Meridian shortly after he did, each from Gulf War carrier squadron assignments. Ted had flown his required combat missions and received a Bronze Star, Air Medal, and appropriate credit in his record. With his contacts, the O'Haras of this world were no threat to him. Rusty, a reserve officer, would be accepted into the Regular Navy when he applied. His Distinguished Flying Cross would earn that for him, but Rusty would never, Ted thought, become an admiral.

The lone sentry saluted and waved him out the air station gate and into the darkness. Few cars passed him on the road from the station in the clear, starry night. He looked at his watch. Still time to make a call when he arrived home.

Chapter Eight

Six weeks after Allison arrived at Meridian, a new draft
of jet-phase flight students, including three women, arrived
from primary training at Pensacola. The squadron operations officer, Lieutenant Commander Al Cronin, assigned
primary flight instructors. Allison's eyes narrowed when
she saw the list.

As she walked down the passageway toward Cronin's
office, Allison reminded herself that her anger must be
carefully controlled, her response respectfully measured.
Lieutenants (junior grade) did not barge in and chew out
lieutenant commanders. Not more than once.

She'd first met Cronin at the Friday afternoon gathering
after her arrival. A cool, detached character about ten years
older, with a long, studious, expressionless face and a pipe
in his hand, Cronin had asked about her ambitions. He'd
only nodded when she said she intended to fly fighters.
After reflection, and what she'd heard about Cronin, the
idea must have blown his mind.

Cronin's office was full of papers piled and strewn. He
looked up when she came in, but did not rise from behind
the mound of documents.

"Commander, I need to talk to you, please." By regulation, she could have called him Mr. Cronin, but she gave
him the more facile courtesy instead.

"Go ahead," he said, and waved his pipe. His eyes returned to the paperwork.

45

"I have acquired all three women students among the incoming draft," she said.

"That's right, Douglas," he replied without looking up. Using her last name reminded her she was a subordinate. Pre-Vietnam naval officers addressed enlisted subordinates that way, she'd heard. Cronin didn't have that excuse. Directed toward an officer, Allison regarded such address as arrogance verging on insult.

"Is there some reason I was given all of them, sir?"

"There doesn't have to be a reason," Cronin mumbled. He continued to work on the papers, still without offering her a seat.

"Let me rephrase the question, sir. I have all three of the incoming women students. I'm not sure that's a coincidence."

"So what, Douglas. What are you trying to say?" He puffed on the pipe and looked at her again, this time letting his gaze linger in a way that made her uncomfortable.

"The black students aren't all being assigned to Bob Little," she said quietly, making Cronin strain slightly to hear her mention one of the squadron's three black instructor pilots. Cronin's expression changed.

"What was that, Douglas?"

Her soft voice might have spelled reticence, hesitance, or uncertainty, she thought.

"I said the black students aren't all being assigned to Bob Little, sir!" She had raised her voice, since he insisted, enough to be heard in the room outside through the open door.

Cronin stood up suddenly, facing her across the desk. Gaunt and tall, his height looked down at her. "What does that have to do with the assignments?" His voice remained soft, but the tone became tense. His face hardened into a scowl.

"Perhaps you can tell me, sir. I don't understand why you made all three of these assignments to me. Before I take these students up and put them through a long training cycle and a wring-out, I'd find it useful to know why I have all three women.''

"What do you mean by a wring-out, Douglas? I'm not sure I understand the term.''

Her arm and neck muscles tensed. Cronin was playing hardball to make her lose her cool. She wasn't fool enough to play his game.

"I would wash out any of those women as quickly as anyone else if they don't measure up.''

"That's your job. So what's the big deal, Douglas? You don't make sense. Do you mean you want someone else to wash out the women who can't hack it?''

Allison felt the color rise in her face. She boiled inside but avoided the obvious retort, wondering how often her father had to put up with jerks like this.

"I've already answered that, sir. The present assignment list segregates part of the class and leaves questions that are difficult to answer these days.'' Allison remained cool, and standing. Cronin still hadn't offered her the courtesy of a seat.

"Segregates, Douglas? My, but you do have a way with words. Are we next to expect Women's Lib picketing outside the gate, telling us how to assign our women personnel?''

"No, sir,'' she said, wanting to bite her lip. "Treating any defined group of students differently in the training process raises unnecessary questions about why.'' Her eyes riveted on Cronin so strongly that she forced him to look at her.

"Talk straight. You're implying malicious prejudice, aren't you, Douglas? That's a serious accusation. You'd better be prepared to back it up.''

"No such implication, sir. I'm simply pointing out that these assignments will raise questions later, if there's an unforeseen problem. Instructors would be easy to change now, without attracting attention. Were something to happen later, this coincidence would be more difficult to explain, unless there's some totally valid operational reason I don't know about.''

"What sort of unforeseen problem do you mean, Douglas? Is this a threat?'' Cronin puffed more rapidly on the pipe. "Or don't you want anything to do with training women pilots?''

"I see no advantage to any one instructor training *all* the women pilots, or all the black pilots, or all the Hispanic pilots, or all the Asian-American pilots, Commander. If there is some reason that's useful, I'd appreciate it if you'd share it with me.''

Cronin's face reddened.

"You're not paid to schedule instructor assignments. I'll worry about 'advantages.' You ignored my question, Douglas. What's going to happen later?''

Her answer began with a shrug. "You tell me, Commander. You've been training pilots longer than I have. What I do know is that there's less question about whether women receive preferential treatment if they're dispersed among a range of instructors.''

Her eyes remained riveted on him, as they had been since she entered the room. Except for the one discomfiting gaze, Cronin had avoided looking at her.

"You're making a big deal out of nothing. I haven't time to play games about this.'' He waved his hand and seemed ready to dismiss her.

"Sir, we seem to have a difference of opinion we can't resolve. I request your permission to discuss this with the executive officer.'' The "request" was a polite formality. Regulations gave her the right to redress a grievance with the executive officer, or XO, whether or not Cronin approved.

"Talk to whomever you want, Douglas, but there's no sense wasting valuable time over nothing,'' he said, puffing on the pipe again. Cronin reached for the assignment roster, scratched on it for a moment, and handed it to Allison.

"Now you've got all red-meat young male student pilots," he said. "I hope you're satisfied. Don't ask me to change this again if you don't like the way one of them parts his hair." Allison ignored the verbal slap.

"Thank you, sir. I'm sure this will work out better for everyone."

"Unless there's something else, I'm busy. You may go, Douglas," he said, dismissing her. Allison turned and walked toward the door. She wanted to jam Cronin's wings up his nose.

"Douglas, a bit of advice," his voice said from behind her. "It doesn't pay to be too much of a fighter." Allison knew it would be wiser to let him have the last word. But after the way he'd treated her, she decided not to. She turned on her heel and looked directly at him.

"I thought the Navy expected aviators to fight—and win, Commander. Perhaps I have it wrong ... sir," she responded, then turned away without waiting for an answer.

As Allison walked down the passageway, she tried to calm the frantic beating of her heart. She didn't see Rusty—coming toward her in a flight suit, his hair tousled, face smiling—until he spoke.

"Hey, Chip, why so glum?"

The comment startled her. His cheerful face was a welcome sight.

"Sorry, Rusty, I've had a bad morning."

"Let's fix it over lunch. We're not flying this afternoon. Let's bust loose and go into town. My stomach's ready to go AWOL on officers' club food."

The tension began to leave her. She smiled back at him. "Sure," she said. "That sounds great."

"Pizza?" he said tentatively. "We'll run the cholesterol off on the track this afternoon."

Rusty treated her like any other pilot, more as a flying buddy than a woman. She was happy about that, but knew it wouldn't go on for long. Pretension was not part of his nature. No *pâté de fois gras,* vintage wine, or cucumber sandwiches with Rusty, she thought. No concealing his feelings for long, either.

"Okay, let's do it," she said.

The tall, extra-large soda tasted good to Allison after the long drive into town, and took the edge off her prickly confrontation earlier that morning.

"What is it with Cronin, Rusty?" she said.

O'Hara's smile disappeared, his lips a thin, tight line now. He leaned forward toward her.

"So that's what's eating you. Did you have a run-in with him? Did he make a pass—"

"Wait a minute," she interrupted. "I only want to know what makes him tick. He assigned me as primary instructor for all three of the women in the incoming class. I think he did that to isolate the women, to discredit all of us if a problem arose. I called him on it. He backed off only when I threatened to go to the XO. Cronin's sore, of course, and he'll get even with me if he can. I think the man has a pathological prejudice against women aviators."

"He didn't do anything else, say anything else to you?"

"If he did, he'd be in the hospital and I'd be in the brig."

Rusty laughed and slapped the rough pine top of the table.

"Good for you, Chip, but we should all remember to keep our tempers in check."

She took another sip of the frosty drink.

Rusty continued. "Cronin went through a bad divorce last summer. His wife walked out, taking most of the furniture when he was on a three-day cross-country training hop. They'd had other problems. She'd called the police a few months before, claiming he'd beat her up. There were rumors about loud arguments, broken furniture. Now she's in Toledo, or is it Cincinnati? Cronin's an . . . unhappy man, but it looks to me like he brought it on himself. I wouldn't give you a plugged nickel for his promotion chances, either, based on the police complaint and his job reputation. You're sure he didn't make a run on you?"

Rusty's expression suggested that he was ready to tear Cronin apart.

"Not even close. I think he hates women, and I'm sure of it now that you've told me his pathetic story. He won't get away with taking his prejudices out on the entire female population, and that includes the students. I can stand up to Cronin, and I will. *They* can't. Cronin won't ever try to make a run on *this* aviator."

"Finish your soda and maybe we'll have some salad, if you'd like that better. We can pass on the pizza and have a big batch of rabbit food if you'd prefer."

His warm hand on her shoulder as he reassured her about Cronin felt good. His touch was gentle, not at all now as though she were merely a flying buddy. Rusty was beginning to remind her of Michael. *Careful,* she thought. *Be very careful.*

"That would be very nice, Rusty," she said, clasping his hand briefly before he took it away.

Chapter Nine

When Allison returned to the BOQ about 2:00 P.M. after work, a message from Ted Chadwick invited her to dinner the following evening. Ted may have seen her leave the base with Rusty, and he probably wanted to see if his options remained open.

Allison changed into exercise gear for her daily run. She'd begged off on running this afternoon with Rusty. She wanted time to think, and jogging provided the opportunity. No telephones, no students, no complexities of flight—simply time alone when stresses, mental and physical, could be whittled down to size.

As she ran along the back streets of the base, she reckoned that Ted's invitation kept Rusty and her from looking too much like a couple. As with most bases, word circulated around NAS Meridian quickly. No woman aviator could have a button missing without half the base knowing about it.

Perspiration trickled down her midriff from the exertion. Michael *would* have wanted her to go on, to find happiness. She'd have wanted the same thing for him if *her* T-39 had gone down. Everything and everyone had told her to make a life for herself outside flying. Jogging every day, harder and longer than necessary, had kept her impulses in check, but she was young, healthy, and unattached. This couldn't go on forever.

After a hot shower in the BOQ, Allison decided it was time to stop mourning and get on with her life. She wouldn't put Michael's picture away, but neither would she live only the tender, beautiful memories she had with him.

Rusty strategically happened by at a good time to go to dinner. He had acquired CDs of Beethoven's nine symphonies and wanted her to listen to a couple of them afterward.

"I didn't know you were into classical," she said.

"Beethoven, Brahms, and Bach do not a classical guru make, but I like some of it. Most Wagner puts me to sleep or gives me a headache. I like Vince Gill and Clint Black a lot, too. Anyway, this Beethoven's Ninth will melt your mascara," he smiled.

"Considering I don't wear any, that might be quite a trick," she said. She did like the music, and whether they looked like a couple or not, dinner in town was part of the game tonight.

The tiny, family operated Chinese place on the far side of town specialized in Szechuan. The clients were mostly Asian-American. The food was peppery, crisp, fresh. One tiny red pepper started a five-alarm fire in her mouth until Rusty came to the rescue with ice water. After a year in San Diego, she should have known about those little rascals, she thought. Both laughed, but she didn't taste much after that.

Darkness had fallen when they came out of the restaurant and walked toward the car.

"Allison," he said. Surprised to be suddenly called by her real name, she turned toward him. They were between cars, not far from their own, hidden from view. A light, warm breeze blew along the deserted street.

"You're a super lady," Rusty said. He took her head in his hands and kissed her firmly but gently. She didn't push him away, only put her hands lightly on his arms. No longer was she just another aviator named Chip, she thought. Now she was Allison, the woman. And Rusty showed signs of being a pretty exciting kisser.

"Are we still on for Beethoven?" he whispered.

"Only if you play the Third and the Fifth after that Ninth," she said.

"You drive a hard bargain, but we can do it."

Later, they sat in the subdued lighting of his BOQ room, holding hands while the commanding tones of Beethoven boomed through Rusty's sound system. When she closed her eyes, Allison imagined sitting in a concert hall, the sixty-piece orchestra only a few rows away.

Rusty, his arm around her, made no move to force her hand. She stretched her head back, feeling comfortable just to be with him. He did, however, give her one very warm, lingering kiss, which she didn't resist.

Earlier that week, Ted Chadwick called a friend at Miramar. His Naval Academy classmate, fighter pilot "Socks" O'Keeffe, was very helpful.

"Allison Douglas had a boyfriend cum fiancé named Mike Nelson here," O'Keeffe said. "Big romance, maybe marriage in the sights. He was the F-14 driver who crashed several months ago at sea. You may remember the incident—they never found his body. She has a mind of her own. The woman wants to be a fighter pilot, no less. Are you making a run on her?"

"Just checking, Socks. We're having dinner this week. Thought I'd learn enough to be smart. Losing her boyfriend that way cuts some subjects out of the conversation. Really appreciate the input, buddy."

It was none of Socks' business that he indeed intended a run. As he hung up the phone, Chadwick considered ways to cut O'Hara out of the pattern. Based on how long ago Nelson had died, he estimated, Allison should be about ready to rejoin the dating world now.

Chapter Ten

Back in her BOQ room after the rousing Beethoven and Rusty's good-night hug and kiss, Allison stretched out on the bed to think. More attractive men filled her life than she knew what to do with. Rusty and Ted were two with the most active interest, but not the only prospects. The squadron and the base abounded with attractive bachelors. She'd have to choose one day. Not right away, of course.

Cora Cochrane was the only friend she could talk to about such things, someone with experience twenty years richer, a sensible, sincere person she could trust. Cora would give her good advice, and keep quiet about it—almost like having her mother back.

Tomorrow Ted might invite her to his apartment in town for after-dinner coffee. The outcome of that evening might tell her something.

She slipped into a nightgown, brushed her teeth, and turned in.

The next thing she knew, she dreamed she was in a T-2C jet trainer, flying along in a blue sky on what appeared to be a routine "hop." Without warning, the engines went silent. For a long moment, the plane continued in straight, level flight, then started to plunge. She had to get out. But there was a student up front. First, she must get him out. The dive became steeper; she tried to push the canopy back, but it was stuck. The stick wouldn't respond. The airplane tumbled end over end. The ground raced up, faster and faster. Then trees and grass flashed before her.

Suddenly everything went dark, and she awoke sitting up, her skin clammy and her body shaking. The clock read four-fifteen A.M.

Allison sat on the side of the bed for a few minutes until the tremors subsided. She stripped off her damp nightgown, took another from the dresser, and slipped it over her head. The dry warmth reassured her. She sat in the chair to gather her thoughts.

Unlike her relationships with men, which she could discuss with Cora, she could talk to no one about this without the risk of being grounded, especially in a training command. They'd never tolerate an instructor with shaky nerves. The flight surgeon and the shrink would ground her until they analyzed her problem. Perhaps there'd be a notation in her medical record. The dream would be blown out of proportion in their effort to avoid a mistake. Cronin would love it, she thought, if she were grounded, even transferred out.

She wondered what the dream was trying to tell her. Never had her confidence in flying wavered. The T-2C was one of the safest airplanes in the Navy's inventory.

Sleep evaded her. She'd make a cup of coffee, maybe take her run early, as the sun came up. The dream was an aberration, perhaps from something exotic in the Chinese food last night. Spices could do funny things to people. It couldn't be a reaction to Rusty's firm kiss, or his hug when they said good night.

She thought about the dream as she jogged through the base in the cool half-light of a budding dawn. The normal glow of exertion was welcome after the ominous, uncontrolled clamminess of fear. The run would sweat this whole thing out of her, Allison thought.

After morning paperwork at the squadron, she went to the training aids library and pulled out the voluminous NA-TOPS safety manual for the T-2C and reviewed bailout and safety procedures in case of engine failure. Assurance that she had the rules down tight made her feel better. After this, she would double-check the canopy in her airplane, do even more thorough preflights, and spend more time talking to the enlisted mechanics.

The day's flying passed uneventfully, through ideal fall weather and sunny skies, with a bright, competent student who loved to fly. She was grateful each day, she thought, to be in a cockpit instead of bound to a desk somewhere.

On her way back to the BOQ, she wondered what Ted might do now that he'd known her for a while. After showering, Allison looked at herself in the mirror. She liked what she saw—a firm, fit figure, trim and lean but with gentle feminine curves. She selected a pleated skirt and a long-sleeved, loose-fitting blouse.

Their dinner conversation at a seafood house in town focused on aviation business, T-2s, and students.

"I'm really curious. Why do you want to fly fighters, Allison?" Ted asked.

"Fighter and attack airplanes are the top of the line, the greatest professional challenge. Why be less than the best? Congress and the Defense Department will eventually understand that women can fly combat aircraft as capably as men."

Ted shifted slightly in his chair and nodded. His expression didn't change.

She didn't mention her former admiral's recommendation for test pilot school. To test new aircraft that a generation of fighter and attack pilots would fly for years afterward would be especially exciting. Some self-styled hotshots in her squadron had no such recommendation, she thought. No sense in rubbing it in. Before that, though, she'd have to prove herself in the fleet and gain experience with the big jets.

"My father keeps a sharp eye out for aviation talent," Ted said. "He's helped many promising aviators into the right flying billets. His talent search has been good for everyone concerned."

Ted could obviously influence the process. She wondered

how many women aviators Vice Admiral Chadwick had
helped.

Others Allison knew had painted Ted's father as a cal-
culating politician with little interest in the people serving
under him. This was no time to foreclose options, she
thought, but her life and career would continue to advance
on her terms. Politics, sexual or otherwise, she reckoned,
were something she'd rather avoid.

Ted invited her to his place after dinner, ostensibly to
show her apartment options near town. Expensive furnish-
ings, oil paintings, and antiques graced the tastefully decorated apartment. The large two-bedroom flat included a
den in the second bedroom, its wall covered with photos,
diplomas, and certificates. Ted, while urbane and polite,
had a large ego. She noticed no pictures of women except
those in his family.

His bedroom contained expensive fruitwood furniture, a
king-size bed, and a massive television. A smaller TV sat
in the living room.

The music was as soft as the lighting when they sat to
talk. He offered her a cognac. She'd tried brandy once and
decided it would make good rocket fuel. Decaf coffee
would let her sleep well after her unscheduled early rise,
she thought, so she opted for that.

"Do you like sailing?" Ted asked. "I have some friends
who keep a boat not far from here, up on the Okatibbee
Reservoir. We could take her out."

"I'd enjoy that," she said, not wanting to admit she'd
never sailed before.

"Like to dance?" he asked. The stereo played a slow,
dreamy dance number.

"I'd love to, Ted, but today was an early up, and I'm
about ready to crash." A bad choice of words, she thought
immediately. "I better go home before I fall asleep on
you."

As they prepared to go out the door to his car, Ted turned

around, almost as though he had forgotten his keys, and faced her.

"Perhaps I'd better say good night here, so the whole base doesn't talk," he whispered.

Before she focused on his meaning, he had wrapped his arms around her. His hands slid up her back and he kissed her firmly while he held her head.

"You're quite a woman, Allison Douglas," he murmured.

Her face felt hot as she was swept into his embrace. His hug was more aggressive than Rusty's. Ted acted more assertive, more sure of himself.

As quickly as his embrace began, it ended. Ted held the door open for her, and she was glad for the fresh air.

As he drove her home, Ted chatted about sailing and repeated his offer, saying he'd arrange something with his friends.

After she closed the door to her BOQ room and prepared for bed, Allison recalled what she'd noticed on a shelf in Ted's bathroom—a woman's gold earring. She had no intention of being one of several women on anyone's string, like a polo pony. If a romance developed between them, she'd make that very clear to him. Far too early now to think about that.

Her sleep that night was dreamless, restful. Before dropping off she remembered the closeness of Ted's embrace, and how she had felt with his arms wrapped around her.

Chapter Eleven

An intensive flying week for students and instructors alike passed quickly for Allison. Tactical instruction in the T2-C introduced the student pilots to the dramatic differences between jet aircraft and the more forgiving propeller planes of basic flight training. When they finished at Meridian, jet aircraft would be as familiar to them as driving a car.

Allison thought it strange she hadn't heard from Rusty for several days; she'd hardly seen him around the squadron. He'd been assigned one of the women flight students in the new draft for jet instruction. Laramie Cox was a slender blond rancher's daughter from Montana, bright and quick. Allison had evaluated Cox as clever. Cox and Rusty, both being rural people, might have things in common.

Ted called Allison on Tuesday night.

"How about a sail this weekend?" he asked.

"I'd like that, but tell me more about it."

"Some married friends have a large sailboat on the reservoir up north. They like to sail on the weekends. You ladies can share one cabin and we boys will share the other."

The other couple would keep things honest, she thought.

"That sounds fine, Ted, but I want to bring some groceries and things, and help with the cooking."

"The cooking? You'll have to help with the crewing, which includes the cooking. If you agree, I think we've got a great weekend ahead."

"Certainly, Ted. When do you want to leave?"

"Saturday morning, early. We usually try to get under way by nine-thirty or ten."

Heavy thunderstorms were sweeping the lower part of the state, grounding flying for the next day and a half and forcing instructors to double up on the already-heavy flying schedule. Friday afternoon arrived quickly. She would pack and shop tonight for the weekend.

The drive to Lake Okatibbee wound through rugged, tree country and into the small town of Martin, and then past it to the reservoir. When they arrived at the boat, a handsome, well-kept thirty-footer with teak decks and gleaming fittings, she saw no other car, no other people.

"Nancy and Hal should be here by now," he said. "They don't live that far away." Allison felt uneasy.

"We need some ice anyway. I'll get that and call them from the marina," Ted said.

"Shall I go along?" she offered.

"No need. Stow the groceries in the galley and look around. I'll be back in a few minutes."

She guided herself through the wood-paneled, tastefully decorated sailing yacht, designed for creature comfort rather than speed. No surprise that Ted had wealthy friends. The sleeping accommodations in the small, elegantly appointed cabins were more than comfortable for a weekend sail. Allison looked forward to decompressing.

When Ted returned with the ice, his face showed concern.

"Nancy and Hal Jacobson have to cancel out. Her mother, who lives in Jackson, was taken ill this morning. They're leaving to go over there. They tried to call, but we were already on the way up here."

She remained silent.

Ted continued, "Hal said we should go ahead and take the boat. It's an easy sailer. Should still be fun, although I'm sorry you won't get to meet the Jacobsons this time."

He had assumed that going out with him alone for the

weekend would be all right. She might look prudish to back out now. After all, she reasoned, there were two cabins. On the other hand, it seemed too coincidental that the Jacobsons backed out at the last minute.

With his carefully groomed Navy career on the line, Ted wouldn't force himself on a woman officer, especially after the Tailhook scandal. Why cancel a nice weekend because something *might* happen? Her delay in responding must be obvious to him.

"I'm sorry too. I hope her mother will be all right. Which cabin would you like?" she said. Ted showed no overt reaction.

"You take the one midships," he said. "It has the plumbing. The one forward is smaller, but still comfortable. If you're ready to learn how to be a *real* sailor, I'll split the hard parts with you."

After a half-hour's preparation, they cast off onto the large lake. A light breeze carried them easily to the center. He tacked the boat north, teaching Allison to handle sail as he steered and captured the wind. They anchored for a brief lunch, then examined coves and inlets and the shoreline during the afternoon.

By 5:00 P.M. they'd reached a remote, forested cove, sheltered from the wind, where the yacht rode easily at anchor. Ted was an accomplished sailor. Midshipmen learned sailing at the Naval Academy, she recalled.

"Ahoy," he said, "the sun is officially over the yardarm." When she looked up, he was there with an iced bottle of Cordon Rouge champagne in a silver bucket with two crystal glasses.

"Too much of that and your cook might mess up dinner tonight," she said lightly, a reminder that she drank very little.

"This is magic bubbly. It only makes you happy, nothing else." Ted was almost believable.

She still didn't swallow the cancellation story about the other couple. After just a couple of sips, her head felt light.

He came over to her chair and knelt down beside her, his face close to hers.

"It's been a wonderful day," he said, kissing her lightly beneath her ear. He seemed ready to linger there a while.

"I'd better start dinner," Allison said as she stood and headed toward the galley. They'd agreed to divide the cooking chores, and she had drawn the dinner.

Ted came out with a frosty bottle of Anjou rosé to complement her dinner of fresh shrimp and crab sauté with herbs. The glow of sunset lighted the lake as though it were on fire, outlining trees against the sky. Birds flew by near the shore, skillfully catching the air currents. The sound of water gently lapping against the hull blended with the mating calls of lake birds along the shore.

Ted poured the wine into crystal stems as they dined on a table set near the stern of the yacht. When the sun finally faded, a small oil lamp lit the table. He tuned romantic music on the stereo system. The soft, relaxed mood made the busy world of airplanes and students dissolve with the sunset.

She could do worse than Ted Chadwick, Allison thought as the music, the mood, and the dinner combined to relax her. The wind, sunshine, and rigging the sails had produced a pleasant tiredness.

A light breeze made the boat rock gently. The evening air was cool and sweet. He took her hand, signaling her to stand up. As they began to dance, Ted moved closer. She felt his strong arms and his warm breath on her neck, smelled his expensive cologne. This was the first time since Michael that she had danced.

The dreamy music and the evening breeze was hypnotic, but dangerous. He began to kiss the side of her neck softly as they danced, lightly and without pressure. He put his head next to hers, nuzzling her gently. The gesture felt pleasant, but her mind returned to the lone woman's earring in Ted's apartment. When his kisses became more numerous and artful, she knew it was time to stop.

"Ted, can we sit down for a while?"

The night was dark and clear, with stars that resembled diamond chips on black velvet. He started to pour more rosé into her glass, but she declined with a motion of her hand.

"You're fascinating, Allison, in many ways. Women with your sense of adventure are rare."

His voice sounded cultured and warm, more sincere and closer in the darkness. Nightfall made everything more intimate, she thought.

"I'm not adventurous at all," she said. "I'm boringly conventional except that I like to fly. I like you too, Ted, but let's take it easy. There was an aviator, at Miramar. We were about to be engaged when he was killed. I'm still getting over that."

"I'm sorry, Allison. I understand how you feel." He leaned over to kiss her cheek in the darkness, took her hand in his again, and rubbed the back of it lightly with his finger. "Some things mustn't be rushed," he said.

She knew there would be no rushing her. This relationship would be different from the one with Michael, if anything developed. Ted stood further back from things. His emotions and aggressiveness were carefully controlled. Aviation didn't have the same urgency for him as it had for Michael, or for that matter, for Rusty and herself.

"It's been a wonderful day, Ted. This is a great place to sail," she said, trying to change the subject.

"We must come up here again. It's a wonderful getaway from life at Meridian. There are other good spots around I think you'd also like."

"The peace and quiet here are wonderful," she said, resisting further commitment now. The night and the weekend weren't over yet, and she'd be sleeping on a boat alone with Ted, albeit in different cabins. Had his friends lent him the boat for overnight sails with other women? Allison thought of the owner of the earring. She knew what it would look like if word got around the base that they'd been alone on a boat for the weekend. No one would believe the outing had been innocent. Only Ted knew, however. Only he could tell where they'd been. If he did, that would be the end.

They talked for another half hour, until she grew sleepy. The little wine she'd had was more than usual, she thought—more than she should have had. The sun, fresh air, and the wine was a formula for sound sleep. More, she thought, would be a recipe for disaster.

Ted embraced and kissed her before she stepped down below. She quickly slipped into her cabin. With the deadbolt locked on the cabin door, she changed into her nightgown in the darkness. Allison fell asleep to the gentle motion of the boat and the rhythmic sound of water against the hull.

Chapter Twelve

Allison awoke to the smell of bacon cooking in the nearby galley. Her watch said seven-fifteen. She dressed and splashed water on her face and ran a brush through her hair.

Ted had set the table back aft; coffee bubbled on the small galley stove.

"You're up early," she said, surprising him.

"Lying in bed with your eyes open is a waste of time," he said. "Thought I'd get up and practice my gourmet cooking, make a good breakfast before we go back."

He put the spatula down, kissed her lightly on the forehead, and went back to work. Nice touch, she thought.

"How do you like your eggs?"

"Over easy, thanks."

She felt a slight tension between them. Ted had wanted last evening to end differently. He might expect faster progress with women he dated, especially in such romantic settings. But it wasn't her problem, she decided.

"How about a swim after breakfast settles down?" he asked. Large, fluffy towels were among the amenities in the cabin. A small marine shower would let her wash up after they returned.

"Good idea," she said.

"Go ahead and change. I'll finish the dishes."

She'd packed a comfortable one-piece green suit. When she returned, Ted had washed the dishes and pots from the previous evening, an unexpected touch.

The lake water was cool and deep, cold enough to wash away mental cobwebs. Both strong swimmers, Ted and Allison struck out for shore, where a shallow beach a few hundred yards away offered a private place for sunbathing. Once on the beach, Ted took her hand. They walked its length for a quarter-mile, then returned to where they had come ashore. The yacht rode easily at anchor nearby in the cove.

He took her hand as they sat and talked on the narrow strip of sand, trees behind them and the lightly rippling lake before them. Clouds glided slowly by. The remote natural environment was powerfully attractive. He kissed the back of her hand, then opened her palm.

She felt the light touch of his lips in the soft center of her hand, before he gently closed it. Ted had been a gentleman so far, she thought, but something told her that his patience with her had been carefully calculated.

They returned to the boat an hour later. On the return trip, she took the helm. She was learning the new skill easily while Ted handled the sails.

The return voyage provided time to think. He could have come on stronger last night or this morning, she thought, but he didn't. Ted was charming, and quite attractive. She enjoyed going out with him, but she was skittish about any kind of involvement. It was still so soon after Michael. And she didn't want to kick Rusty out of the picture. Oddly enough, she found herself drawn to thoughts of the sweet guy with the red hair.

Ted interrupted her musings. "I have some great filets at home ready to go. Why not come over and I'll put a quick dinner together?"

She shook her head. "Ted, thanks for a wonderful weekend, but I'm behind on everything to get ready for this week. With last week's flying schedule and our sailing plans, I'm guilty on multiple counts of procrastination in the first degree. It's my fault. Perhaps another time soon. Will you give me a rain check?"

"My pleasure," he said, taking her hand now. "Let's do something else like this again soon."

She said good-bye with warm thanks for the weekend, and a friendly kiss.

Rusty, late for an appointment, almost ran her down in the passageway of the squadron administration building. He looked distracted. He apologized and offered dinner that evening, saying he needed to talk to her, as he ran off down the hall.

Later, over dinner, Rusty spoke of Laramie Cox.

"Her record says she did fine in the T-34 propeller phase, but she's not hacking it with the T-2," he said, his face a mask of frustration. "In jets, it's like she's never flown an airplane before. She clutches up, loses her nerve."

"Rusty, the T-34 is a forgiving airplane. The switch to the T-2 is a real transition. Different handling, higher landing speeds, tougher, faster tactics, the whole thing. I took a while to get used to it when I went through." She wouldn't make excuses, she thought, but she didn't want Rusty to downcheck a student prematurely.

Some male aviators would have simply let Laramie bilge out. Rusty would at least give Laramie the benefit of the doubt, as he would anyone else.

"Take her up for a check-ride and tell me what you think," he said. "You work differently with the students than I do. Perhaps your way will work better with her."

Allison scheduled Laramie up in a T2-C trainer, the standard advanced training aircraft used for student carrier qualifications. The T-2 was easier to fly than the T-A4C, the older training version of a Vietnam-era attack bomber.

As she did the paperwork, Allison thought back to her own first carrier landing. *You can get killed,* she'd thought, *if you screw up, don't know, aren't sure, lose nerve.*

An hour of aerial training maneuvers with Ensign Cox convinced her that Rusty was right.

"Laramie," she said, "you've got to get your landing speed down and come in slower, more gradually."

"Let me try it again," Laramie replied. Her voice wavered.

She'd faltered several times during touch-and-go landings on the simulated flight deck runway. She made critical decisions too late, overcorrecting dangerously late more than once. Had this been a tense foul-weather carrier landing such as her own first solo approach to *Forrestal*, Allison thought, Laramie Cox would be dead. Unless she improved or was bilged out, Laramie would kill herself and some flight deck people and destroy a multimillion-dollar aircraft.

"Laramie, you have a real problem with landing jets," she said as they walked from the flight line back to the hangar. Allison wasn't impressed with the rest of her flying either. Rusty had been more than charitable.

Laramie's face looked tense and worried, her earlier facade of confidence now eroded. "I can do it, Lieutenant McCoy. Adapting to jets is taking longer than I thought, but I'll get the hang of it. I've got to make it through."

Rusty was smart, she thought, to give Laramie an impartial check-ride with a female instructor immune to any boy-girl influences the attractive Laramie might foster. Allison hadn't foreseen this situation during her confrontation with Cronin weeks before. Now she knew she'd been right to avoid becoming mother hen for the female students. Allison was also convinced Laramie should not advance to the carrier landing stage.

Rusty had other things to talk about over their next dinner together, but kept the subject on the student aviator as long as Allison wanted to.

"I have a bad feeling about Laramie, Rusty. Her landings were marginal, at best."

O'Hara's brow wrinkled. He hunched forward toward her. "It's not just me, then," he said.

"No," she replied. "You described her flying accurately, down to the last detail. She can't handle jets." Allison didn't mention that instinct told her that Laramie would try anything to succeed.

"Maybe she'd do better in helicopters," he said. "Jets aren't for everyone. Helicopter pilots require special aptitudes too. Perhaps that will turn out to be her niche." Both know Laramie had to complete the jet-phase curriculum here in order to get her wings.

"Do you think she'll solo the T-2?" Allison said. "What if she gets to carrier qualifications and freezes up? If she doesn't bingo into the beach, and tries to bring the plane aboard and crashes, whose fault will that be?" She remembered her own concerns even when she knew she could handle the aircraft.

"Rusty, I'm ready to tell Cronin that I think she should be screened for disenrollment. The process will take lots of paperwork, and it should be started early, like now."

"I'll talk to him first," Rusty said. "Laramie's my student. Given the facts, I shouldn't have a problem convincing even Cronin that she's an accident about to happen."

To recommend that a student be dropped was the toughest part of life for an instructor. Formal disenrollment was ultimately approved by the commodore himself, Commander Air Training Wing One.

When they met for lunch the next day, Rusty's face looked almost as red as his hair. His voice shook with barely controlled anger as he told her that Cronin had all but thrown him out of his office.

An hour later, Allison stood in front of Lieutenant Commander Cronin in his office.

"So, Douglas, you take Ensign Cox up for an hour and decide she's ready for disenrollment." Cronin seemed even more abrasive than usual, she thought.

"It's not my place to decide anything, Commander. My comment is a heads-up, a recommendation to consider. We shot six touch-and-go landings. Every one was white-knuckles. I had to take the stick away from her twice."

"Aren't you overdramatizing this? After all, she's not that far into jet phase," Cronin responded.

"If she can't handle a T2-C with an instructor, she can't take a C-2, an S-2, or anything else with a tailhook aboard ship. At this rate, Ensign Cox will kill herself when she attempts her first solo CARQUAL landing."

"Douglas, we have a hundred thousand dollars' worth of training invested in Ms. Cox at this point. Disenrolling her would be an expensive loss for the U.S. government. Why not give her additional coaching and the chance to acquire more experience? I'll ask the CO to authorize more flying hours."

What was it with Cronin? she wondered. Why should he, male chauvinist extraordinaire, be so protective of a woman aviator?

"Ensign Cox will one day soon destroy a multimillion-dollar aircraft and kill other Navy people in addition to herself," Allison said. "The training cost argument won't stand against that. If I'm wrong, the screening process will correct me. She may be a perfectly fine helicopter prospect, but I can't judge that. I suggest, sir, a board entirely within standard procedure. Lieutenant O'Hara can provide a detailed analysis based on many more flight hours with her. I defer to his greater experience."

Allison knew she was stuffing Rusty's wartime flying record up Cronin's nose. She thought she sounded the way her father would.

"Well, you and O'Hara keep working with her and see if you can't fix the problem. She might snap out of it and become a 4.0 aviator. Give her another month. If she's not improved by then, we'll take another look. That will be all, Douglas." She didn't like his summary dismissal any more this time than she did previously.

Rusty reacted immediately when Allison told him that evening.

"What is the matter with Cronin? He'll get Cox killed

if he keeps dithering. I've got to go back in and persuade him that she's a danger to herself and others.''

"He'll tell you the same thing he told me, Rusty. We'll have to go to paper, and that will tick him off. He's a vindictive type, and he has it in for me, for starters.''

"Why? What did you do to him?''

"I'm a woman wearing a flight suit. And I speak my mind about important things.''

"You're sure that's all?''

"That's the way I see it. I told you about my last confrontation with Cronin over the women students. Nothing's changed.''

O'Hara sighed and paused for a moment, his brow furrowed.

"Okay, Allison, here it is. No varnish, no bull. Laramie has known for a couple of weeks that she's in deep weeds. She rubbed her hand on my knee in the T2-C the other day in a way that wasn't funny. She wants her wings real bad.''

"Perhaps she wants *two* things too badly.''

"Nah, she didn't come on to me because of my red hair and charming smile. Laramie could have any number of young men around here.''

Allison went over and put her arms around him.

"You're a good man, Rusty,'' she said, "an awfully good man.''

Rusty put his head next to hers, burying his face in her clean, shiny black hair.

"I don't want Laramie Cox, Allison,'' he whispered. His voice had lost its carefree aviator tone. Who he did want was clear.

"I need some time, Rusty. It's—''

"I know about Mike Nelson,'' he said softly, "and I'm sorry that happened to both of you.''

"How . . . ?''

"We went through advanced flight training together. I read about the crash when it happened, but I didn't learn until last Friday about you and him.''

She couldn't tell Rusty she was in gridlock again, this time between him and Ted.

"Bear with me a little, Rusty. I need time to sort things out."

Chapter Thirteen

Rusty's second session with Cronin a week later had the same result. He'd kept detailed, careful notes. Cronin, however, had persuaded the squadron CO to authorize extra flight hours for Laramie. He must have pointed out, Rusty thought, Laramie's high profile as a woman student, the government's investment in her training, and the fact that her father had been a naval aviator.

The CO might also have perceived an attractive woman and a knowledgeable, influential father. Although unconvinced additional flight instruction would help, he could have authorized the time to prove later that Laramie had every reasonable chance to succeed.

When Rusty arrived at the squadron gathering at the officers' club that Friday, he saw Chadwick already had Allison cornered in conversation. Before he had a chance to talk to her, Allison excused herself. Chadwick sidled over to him.

"How's it going, Rusty? Is that neat little Ensign Cox keeping you occupied in the cockpit?"

"Yes, she's certainly doing that, Ted. A thrill a minute. But many of our students provide that, don't they?"

"Yes, extra instruction sometimes pays off. Practice makes perfect." Chadwick's expression implied other things.

"By the way, Allison and I are going along the Tombigbee River this weekend. Been up there?"

"Not yet. I'll put that on my list," Rusty said.

"We had fun sailing last weekend. I have a boat up on the Okatibbee Reservoir. The weather was great."

Rusty looked at his watch. "Glad you had a good time. I have to buzz off, Ted. Heavy date. See you later. Have a nice weekend."

"Yeah, Rusty, you have a real good one too."

O'Hara finished his beer quickly and left before Allison returned. He'd drive to Jackson on Saturday, perhaps return late Sunday. Perhaps, he thought morosely, he'd get a date for tomorrow night.

When Allison came back, Ted had ordered her a wine spritzer. She looked around.

"Didn't I see Rusty a few minutes ago?" she asked him.

"He had a quick beer and left. Said something about a date tonight."

Allison paused, her face pensive.

"Dinner at Weidman's?" he asked.

"Sounds good," she replied. "Whenever you're ready." As they drove into town near sunset, neither noticed Laramie Cox's car in the carport of Al Cronin's place.

"It's really beautiful in the fall up on the Tombigbee River," he said over dinner. "The scenery is terrific and a romantic little B&B overlooks the river about sixty miles up. We could come back Sunday afternoon, have a leisurely time, enjoy ourselves."

"That sounds terrific, Ted, but I have loose ends to tie up that I've let go for weeks. Perhaps another time, if we can."

Two successive weekends alone together would send Ted the wrong signal. She wondered if Rusty would be on the station this weekend. Perhaps she'd find a way to see him.

Cora had called before she got back, and had invited her and a guest to dinner Saturday night. Although it was ten o'clock, Allison called back and said that she'd come alone.

"I'm surprised that you didn't have one of those handsome young hunks on your arm tonight, Allison,'' Cora said when she opened the door the following evening. ''Few of them would pass up a home-cooked meal.''

''Two of them are flying wing on me and I can't decide. It's harder, after Michael. . . .''

''Listen, life goes on. My George wouldn't want me to sit around and mourn for him. I haven't found the right man yet either, but he'll come along. Perhaps it's neither of those two guys for you. Who knows?''

She knew Cora wouldn't ask who they were, but she volunteered the info. ''They're both in VT-6. One is Rusty O'Hara. The other is Ted Chadwick.''

Cora winced inwardly. Ted's father, Vice Admiral Chadwick, frequently phoned the air training wing commander, known as the commodore. Her boss didn't conceal his frustrations with the demanding three-star. Cora disliked the older Chadwick, and didn't like Ted either. Everything was politics in their family, she thought.

''They're very different men,'' Cora said. ''Each has a bright future. Once the honeymoon's over, what two people have in common matters more than anything else over the long haul.''

To tell Allison that a chief's daughter and an admiral's son came from different worlds wasn't easy. Doug Douglas's daughter had leaped the officer-enlisted barrier. She lived in a different world now, but was new to it. Chadwick had lived there all his life.

''I'm not looking for a husband. Neither do I want a hotshot aviator who'll get himself killed.''

''If you're talking about Rusty,'' Cora said, ''people who earn the DFC are risk-takers. But people change as they get older, become more careful. Some wild-hare fighter pilots mellow out before they make commander. The responsibility of squadron command has a way of doing that. Being married with kids helps too.''

''If they live that long,'' Allison whispered.

''Most of them do, you know. What happened to your

Michael, and to my George in that engine room, were accidents. Besides, these days no one can tell whether a grand romance will last past the end of the tour of whoever gets transferred first.''

When Allison returned to the BOQ late Saturday evening, flowers had arrived from Ted. Rusty's hasty departure from the Friday get-together bothered her. He was usually early to arrive and late to leave. Must have been some important date, she thought.

When Allison called the next morning to thank Ted for the flowers, a sleepy female voice answered. She must have dialed the wrong number, Allison thought. On the other hand, such a mistake wasn't like her. She dialed again. The phone rang a dozen times without answer.

Cora's Monday was slow with the commodore out of town. She called her friend Sophie in Washington, the writer for Ted Chadwick's father. The two chiefs spoke every week, to exchange information about mutual friends and news. Cora said that Ted was working hard in VT-6. A heavy student load, staff reductions, and budget cuts, she said, had made things tighter.

"Ted wants his father to transfer him out of there early, give him a staff job up here," Sophie said. She swore her friend to secrecy. "Chances are he will. That should make his visits to his girlfriend up here easier." Cora's interest piqued.

"Long-distance romances become expensive," Cora said, hoping to draw her out a bit more.

"He's been dating this socialite named Melanie Brousseau for the past year. Her father is a rich surgeon with a big place out near Leesburg. The mother comes from a wealthy Philadelphia family. They have horses, an antebellum mansion, the whole nine yards. There's talk of an engagement if he's transferred up here. I'd bet my next paycheck he comes to Washington early, given how the system works.''

She detested intrusion into people's lives, Cora thought. To tell Allison about Ted's girlfriend meant a nasty letdown, but it would be easier now than after she'd become serious about him. But the whole thing was none of her business, and Allison was a grown woman. But in the end, the thought of Ted using Allison, then dumping her to marry some rich society snob, infuriated her.

She left word for Allison over at the squadron. The two had tea after work.

''I learned something about Ted Chadwick today,'' Cora said, sipping her tea. ''He has a serious girlfriend, an almost-fiancée, in the Washington area.''

Allison paused for a moment before answering.

''Let me guess—some admiral's daughter he can marry to improve his career potential,'' she said, her voice tense.

''Close. A Leesburg, Virginia, socialite. Her father has a big place out there, horses and all.''

''Of course. Admirals have prestige, but not much money. Ted's father is already protecting his career. A rich socialite makes sense. Someone to keep him in the manner to which he has grown accustomed. The horsey set, no less. Nothing like aiming high.''

The four-flusher, Allison thought. That explained Ted's expensive sports car and fine clothes. He had an image to preserve with this woman and her moneyed parents, even if he had to spend every penny.

''I generally don't intrude into other people's business, Allison, but . . .''

''You've saved me a lot of grief, and I'm very grateful. Better than learning a couple of months from now,'' Allison replied.

Cora nodded her assent. She couldn't tell her about Chadwick's possible early transfer. That didn't matter now. What she'd said provided Allison a clear wave-off.

*   *   *

The girlfriend would explain Ted's cross-country training flights to Andrews Air Force Base, Allison thought as she drove home. He wasn't going home to see his family after all. Her wrong-number phone call to his apartment seemed less like a mistake now.

Allison hadn't seen Rusty since Friday. Usually, he found a way to bump into her almost every day at the squadron.

Why hadn't she seen this coming? Her fury with Ted grew. Cora had done the tough but courageous thing in telling her.

After several more days without seeing Rusty, Allison knew that the problem began with his abrupt departure from the club on Friday. She'd left Ted's phone messages unanswered. This was one relationship she'd sever face-to-face. A telephone kiss-off was as much as he deserved, but her father had told her never to take a course of action wanting in courage. Finally, she called Ted and asked him to meet her at the officers' club.

"I've tried to reach you for days, Allison," he said, waiting for her at a table. Ted drank a scotch and water, instead of his usual beer. A frosty glass of vintage chardonnay stood at her place. The bottle with the remainder of the French wine stood in an ice bucket nearby. What was it with this guy and his wine fetish? she thought.

"The flowers were lovely, Ted, but I think we'll have to stop seeing each other."

"Are you angry at me, Allison?" His face had a strange expression, almost as though he'd been expecting this.

"No, Ted, what do I have to be angry about? My life is too complex now. I need time to get myself together. You know one of the big factors."

"Michael is still with us, isn't he?"

"Michael will always be with me, one way or another."

"I thought we were coming to know each other pretty well," he said.

"It's me, Ted, my fault." She wanted to get this over with.

"It's no one's fault. If things sort out, I'll be here."

Allison looked up behind Ted, in time to see Rusty walk into the bar. He had seen her and Ted, she knew, but gave no indication. Rusty looked around as though trying to find someone, then left. Allison wanted to bite her tongue, but now was not the time.

"I'll be in touch, Ted, if anything changes."

He patted her hand lightly. "I must move along," he said, and excused himself. "See you at the squadron tomorrow."

Allison bit her lip as she drove back to the BOQ. The one time she didn't want Rusty to think she was seeing Ted, and it had to be when she was breaking off for good. Rusty might think the two of them had become an item. Only Ted could have planted that idea, she thought. She'd force an excuse to talk to Rusty, even if it appeared she was chasing him. Laramie Cox was one subject she could use.

She rang Rusty's BOQ room, thinking he would be there. Too early yet for dinner. The phone rang twice before he picked it up.

"O'Hara," he said.

"Rusty, it's Allison. I need to talk to you."

"I thought you were talking to Ted Chadwick."

"Rusty, be serious." Her hand tightened around the phone.

"You caught me going out the door. Can we do this another time, maybe next week?"

"How about coffee after work tomorrow? My treat."

"Not sure I can make it. How about if I let you know tomorrow?"

"Okay, Rusty." She sounded hurt.

What she told Ted was true, she thought. Her life *was* becoming more complicated. The discovery of Ted's perfidy coincided with Rusty going cold on her. If she didn't straighten the situation out, it would be a long, hard winter.

Chapter Fourteen

Allison's restless night alternated between strange dreams and wakefulness. The alarm went off at the usual 0530. Her early-morning run would get a wave-off today. She turned over and tried to sleep during the next hour without success.

Fatigue dogged her through the morning, unchanged by strong coffee, and into the afternoon. For once in her life, she simply went through the motions.

Only at 3:45 P.M., minutes before quitting time, did Rusty call. He'd meet her at the club, he'd said. No offer of a ride, a friendly touch that would have typified their relationship a little more than a week ago.

Frosty white wine, instead of coffee, sat at her place when she arrived. Rusty sipped a beer. When she tasted vintage chardonnay, she knew Rusty didn't miss much.

"What's up?" he asked. No quick humor or sparkle in his voice today. Almost, she thought, as though he anticipated bad news.

"I wanted to talk to you about our favorite female flight student," she said.

His expression changed.

"Oh, yes . . . warm and tender little Laramie, my affectionate, knee-rubbing little Laramie," he said. Still no smile. "And how is Ted these days?" He seemed distant, cold.

Allison felt a sting of blind anger and almost lashed back with a smart answer. Instead she raised the glass and took a sip of wine, buying a few seconds to calm herself. Her

81

hand trembled slightly. She hoped Rusty didn't notice.

"What you saw yesterday was me telling Ted Chadwick that I won't see him anymore."

"Perhaps I should ask, how has he been?"

Rusty must hurt inside, she thought. One of them must stay calm.

"Exactly the same as you."

"Well, not exactly. I'm a better aviator, but I guess he's better at sailing and other things."

So Ted *had* told him about the sailing weekend.

"Ted's a good sailor from what I saw weekend before last. The Naval Academy ring-knockers learn it at the trade school. I don't know about other things."

"What about the real subject of our conversation—sweet little Laramie?" he said.

"Wait a minute. I don't know what Ted told you about our sailing weekend, but nothing happened."

"Hey, Allison, you have nothing to explain to me," he said, raising his hands in a resigned shrug.

"Let's get something straight, Rusty. Ted invited me out on a boat with another couple, Nancy and Hal Jacobson. Her mother was taken ill that morning, so they didn't come. Being alone out there with him was not what I'd signed up for. We slept in separate cabins. Nothing went on. If he implied anything different, he's lying."

She wasn't sure whether she was more furious with Ted, Rusty, or herself.

"If nothing went on, and Chadwick didn't make a run on you, why stop seeing him?"

"He's seeing somebody else. When I found that out— bingo. I called his place Sunday morning, and some woman answered."

"So you confronted him with this yesterday?"

"No, I don't owe him any explanations, and I don't need any new enemies. I simply ended it."

Rusty nodded.

"Okay, okay. Let's talk about Laramie Cox," he said.

"We got nowhere with Cronin," she said. "What if he

cuts her more slack after the month is up?''

"I don't think he will. He's already at risk with the CO for recommending the additional flying hours. No matter what happens, we have to write the flight aptitude reports.'' Rusty breathed deeply and continued. ''Those things are a bureaucratic nightmare. I'd rather dogfight with MIG-29s.''

"If another instructor documented her failings, that would make it easier. Laramie knows she's in trouble, and seems ready to use anything to survive,'' Allison said. ''The more instructors who verify her shortcomings, the better.''

She waited for his reaction.

"True. I can tell Cronin that another instructor, one with a low-key approach, might give her a better chance. I get a little intense when people can't learn after hours of instruction. If he suggests you, I'll say you've already made up your mind, that it should be someone new. Let him find someone else, anyone else.''

The next day, Lieutenant Commander Cronin listened to Rusty's argument. He agreed that another instructor would provide Laramie with a better chance. He had no misgivings about the final outcome. Whoever got her as a student would end up with headaches, have to fail her, and write the lengthy justification for it.

Chadwick's reputation as a ladies' man might mean he'd take on Laramie without complaint. When the cut came, Cronin thought, he could blame the instructors and tell her he'd done everything he could. For now, he'd tell her the change of instructors would improve her chances. She wouldn't object to Chadwick. He would be someone she could deal with.

Cronin phoned the hangar and left word for Chadwick to come see him when he returned from flying. It took only a few minutes to convince Chadwick to take Laramie as a student. Cronin approved the change of instructors the same day.

Chapter Fifteen

One part of him said he still loved Allison, Rusty thought as he walked toward the squadron hangar the morning after they met at the officers' club. Another, smaller part doubted her. He'd been too patient. Ted may have given her a big line during the weekend sail, then fueled her rage toward him when Allison discovered he had another woman.

Maybe she'd learned from that mistake. Or maybe, as she'd said, nothing had happened. He wanted to believe her. This strained their relationship, but didn't have to end it, unless that was what she wanted.

He'd made mistakes of his own. Allison was as much an adult as he was, just as fallible. She owed him an answer about the two of them and how they stood, nothing more. But she'd better make up her mind. Love her or not, Rusty thought, he wouldn't wait forever, especially after this.

Rusty was right, Allison thought. As she sat in the squadron office with the week's paperwork, she knew that she'd better fix their relationship quickly. Ted angered and disgusted her now. The change of instructor assignments for Laramie meant that he'd now been given an opportunity to lead himself astray.

She should have seen through Ted earlier. The sports car, expensive clothes, and the glitzy apartment with the king-size bed should have warned her. She'd been dazzled like a schoolgirl by his phony charm. There never was another couple scheduled on their boating weekend.

But for luck, he would have victimized her twice, once by what he did, and then to foreclose forever her options with Rusty. What a fool she'd been.

Her stomach became queasy as her anger rose. She had already lost one good man. Perhaps she'd now lost another because of a foolish attraction to someone she now knew wasn't good enough to clean Rusty's flight gear. The Virginia debutante who wanted to marry Ted had a tougher problem on her hands, however. She just didn't know it yet.

Chapter Sixteen

Okay, Ensign Broderick, roll her out to the end of the taxiway and obtain tower clearance for takeoff.'' Allison spoke by intercom to the student pilot in the front seat of the T2-C as they headed off the NAS Meridian ramp toward the runway.

Broderick, only three years younger than she, taxied the trainer aircraft toward the eight-thousand-foot Runway 18R at NAS Meridian's McCain Field. She scanned the gauges and silently bird-dogged his procedures from the backseat as he maneuvered the thirteen-thousand-pound twin-jet aircraft onto the wide concrete airstrip. Training doctrine encouraged instructors to let student pilots learn by doing, unless a life-threatening emergency arose.

Flying sometimes went from boredom to terror within seconds. Vertigo had seized Allison briefly during early tactical training, inducing a panic from which she'd quickly recovered. After that, and again following Michael's death, she'd focused more attention while flying on small, subtle things before they became big ones. Perhaps Michael had ignored some minor problem in his F-14.

After her bad dream several weeks before, Allison had memorized the *Trawing One In-Flight Guide* and its emergency procedures. She also kept the booklet in one flight suit leg pocket when flying. The NATOPS Pilot's Pocket Checklist, also committed to memory, was in the other.

Hazards of flight, she knew, must never be left to chance. Student pilots were eager to learn the sophisticated high-speed tactics for which naval aviation was either feared or famous, depending on which side you were on. Students thought about the fun part, less about what *might* happen.

Less than a minute later, she studied the gauges as Ensign Broderick coaxed the throttles forward. The whistling whine of the engines became a powerful, blistering roar. Acceleration forced her back into the seat as the aircraft sped down the runway and lifted gracefully into the cloudless afternoon sky. Four thousand pounds of JP-4 jet fuel would provide an hour of twisting and turning in Operating Area 2, fifty nautical miles from the base.

"Beautiful flying weather, Lieutenant Douglas." Broderick's metallic-sounding voice over the intercom focused her on the hour ahead. As the Mississippi countryside dropped away and they began to climb, the afternoon was sunny and clear, the sky cloudless. Her routine gauge check after takeoff showed everything normal. Today should be a milk run. Time with Rusty would come afterward at the officers' club.

"Sure is. We'll get a lot done this afternoon," she replied.

Students like Broderick were a pleasure to fly with. He was capable, alert, and aggressive, everything he was supposed to be. Her student would likely fly an F-14B Tomcat fighter before she would, if she *ever* would. She didn't like that.

"We're in the OPAREA, Lieutenant," Broderick said.

"Okay," Allison replied, "I want you to put the aircraft into a spin and then recover." The drills, the sequence of which was known only to her, continued.

During one tight, banking turn halfway through the flight, she first noticed the slight shudder, a minor vibration in the airframe. Her eyes went immediately to the instrument panel. The port engine oil pressure gauge oscillated wildly. An eerie tingle started at the base of her skull.

"Pull up and level her out, now!" she snapped. "We

have an emergency.'' Within seconds, Broderick had the aircraft flying straight and level.

"Yikes!'' Broderick blurted over the intercom.

Allison knew he'd just seen his instruments. Port engine oil pressure was dropping rapidly. She agreed with his muttered assessment. She knew this afternoon would become what aviators euphemistically called a "character-building experience.''

"Mr. Broderick, this is *not* repeat *not* a drill.'' Her voice was calm, but steely.

"Run 'Engine Failure During Flight' on the port engine.''

She already knew the procedure. The situation wasn't critical enough that she take it away from him . . . yet. Before the young pilot had slowed the engine to idle speed to test it, the vibration became complicated by rough running. If the situation became no worse than this, Allison thought, they'd secure the port engine and limp home.

"I'll take it now, Mr. Broderick,'' she said gently, grasping the controls from the backseat. She didn't feel calm at all. Her fingers trembled as she took the stick, her stomach suddenly tense. This was no time to take chances, even less for possible mistakes.

"Review ejection procedures in case she goes sour.'' By now, Broderick would have pulled the emergency procedures book from his flight suit pocket. Allison cranked the radio to UHF 340.2, the tower frequency. As she spoke, she scanned each of the gauges, trying to assess the problem.

"November Mike Mike, this is Shad 3. We have vibration and rough running in port engine. Intend secure engine and return to base. Request you designate clear runway and provide landing instructions.''

"Roger, Shad 3,'' the soft female voice answered. "Runways are being cleared for your approach. Keep tower advised of your intentions.''

Allison knew the enlisted air controlman first class in the

Meridian tower had punched a series of buttons on her telephone console and picked up the handset. Seconds later, sirens would sound, lights would flash, and massive diesel engines would roar as crash crews scrambled. Fire, crash, and foam trucks and an ambulance would be alongside the runway within a minute. The training squadron and wing commanders would be en route to the flight line.

After her radio call there was a loud bang, a low whine, and thick black smoke suddenly poured from the port engine. Allison hit the engine fire extinguisher switch. The flames went out, but so did the engine. The plane wobbled uncertainly. She kicked up the power on the remaining engine and turned the aircraft in a wide arc toward NAS Meridian.

The luxury of limping back home lasted only a few seconds. As Allison applied power to maintain altitude, the right engine began running rough.

"Oh, come on!" she hissed, looking again toward the gauges.

Starboard engine oil pressure was dropping downward through 40 PSI. Once the engine seized for lack of oil, it was all over. She wasn't about to wait for that.

"Mr. Broderick, run your ejection checklist—now."

"Ejection checklist, roger," the voice said, tense now.

She punched up the radio.

"Mayday, Mayday, Mayday. November Mike Mike this is Shad 3. Port engine shut down. Starboard engine running rough, losing oil pressure. Preparing to eject."

Allison's voice remained steady as she mentally reviewed the ejection procedure. She had drilled herself in it a hundred times, knew it in her sleep. The knowledge didn't stop her intense perspiration or the concern for Broderick and herself. She pointed the aircraft toward an uninhabited area as they prepared to punch out.

"Shad 3, this is November Mike Mike." The calm, confident voice of the air controller belied the deadly seriousness of the situation. "Roger your last transmission. We have you on radar and are scrambling Jolly Green to your location. Activate your beeper upon touchdown.''

Allison had never figured out why the rescue helicopter was called Jolly Green. At this point, she didn't care.

The air controlman punched the telephone console again. Other numbers responded instantly. More people changed their plans in mid-breath. The ready rescue helicopter crew threw sandwiches aside. Within seconds, Oprah Winfrey's television image spoke to an empty ready room. The Naval Air Station, Meridian, Mississippi, had gone to peacetime general quarters.

The training air wing commander, Captain Giles Woodring, grabbed his hat and dashed for his staff car. His driver, twenty years younger, ran to catch up with him.

"Prepare to eject," Allison barked. Now the fun would really begin, she thought as they awaited the explosive shock of the ejection seat. When she pushed the ejection selector button, both would punch out at once. Oil pressure was passing through 15 PSI and falling. Another few seconds would be too late.

Everything had happened in little more than two minutes. The plane, already level and flying slow enough for ejection, was close to stalling and entering an uncontrollable spin.

"Ready, Broderick?" she asked, a tense trill in her voice. She must be sure he was fully prepared, otherwise he risked serious injury during the punch-out. His response took only a couple of seconds, which seemed like forever.

"Ready, Lieutenant," he finally said, his voice shaky.

She hit the ejection selector and tensed for the rocket blast beneath their seats that would catapult them above the dying aircraft. The violent, wrenching shock was familiar. Each military pilot received ejection seat training and periodic recertifications. Nobody did either one for kicks.

Cold air hit her like a block of ice. The seat separated

from her parachute in unreal slow motion. Seconds later, the open chute stopped her free-fall with a gut-wrenching jolt.

Broderick was below and to her left. His chute billowed in the blue sky. So far, so good, she thought. The T-2, trailing black smoke, was in a steep terminal dive. She watched the fireball as it crashed in the operating area, grateful the wreck was far from any place inhabited.

So much for the milk run, she thought as she shuddered through the cold air of ten thousand feet toward the scrubby earth below. The wind carried them well away from the crash site.

As Allison descended through the cloudless blue sky, an enormous nylon parasol spreading above her, she realized that she'd been able to punch out when Michael had not.

The ground rushed toward her now. In seconds, the parachute dropped her into a bruising roll in the rock-strewn Mississippi scrub. The wind at ground level was light. She collapsed the chute and peeled off the harness. Her first thought was of her student. When she looked behind her, she saw he had landed nearby.

A white-faced Broderick limped sheepishly toward her dragging what was probably a sprained ankle, clearly happy to be alive. Dense black smoke billowed skyward toward the horizon, the funeral pyre of the T-2. Allison felt a chill as she thought of how close they'd come. She looked skyward and whispered a brief prayer of thanks.

"Mr. Broderick," she said, mock sharpness in her voice, "one important teaching point I overlooked. The object of this game is to make equal numbers of takeoffs and landings." She showed no sign of the enervating fear that was only now starting to subside. "On second thought," she said dryly, "some days, getting home alive is close enough for government work."

"Sure beats the alternative," Broderick said. His face remained stark white. He smiled gamely, trying to match her wit. "What do you think happened?" he asked, his face now serious. Perhaps he was concerned that he may have done something wrong.

"Whatever it was, you didn't cause it, if that's what you're worried about. Always pay attention to small things. I looked at the gauges after that slight shudder in the engine. If we'd done another roll and that engine quit on us, instead of pulling up when we did, we'd be playing this ball game on a different team by now." She gestured toward the oily cloud. "Remember that."

Broderick's face told her that he'd received the message.

The radio beeper beacon would lead the rescue helicopter to them within a few minutes. Meanwhile, her legs rubbery, Allison sat on a nearby rock.

"I'm going to make you do at least half the paperwork on this," she said, wagging her finger at Broderick. Everyone knew the average stack of paper on an aircraft accident report investigation stood three feet high. Some aviators would fly a marginal aircraft home in order to avoid the task. "By the way," she said with feigned irritation, "you've made me late for dinner. Try not to let this happen again, will you?" After a brief moment of silence, they both laughed.

Chapter Seventeen

Minutes later, Allison watched as the orange and white rescue helicopter whipped over the horizon toward them. The big machine made a noisy, dust-swirling landing on a nearby flat spot in the rural scrubland.

The corpsman leaped out of the dropper as it touched down and ran toward the two pilots. She spoke to each, felt and then bandaged Broderick's ankle, and helped him toward the aircraft.

"You're lucky, Mr. Broderick," the corpsman said. "It's only a sprain. The flight surgeon needs to see both of you after we get back."

Only time would heal the large bruise on her seat that accompanied the hard landing, Allison thought. A cheap price for the afternoon's otherwise expensive adventure.

The helicopter pilot's radio report to the base came through the intercom in the helmet the crew chief had given Allison as he strapped her into a seat.

"November Mike Mike, this is Jolly Green. Both Shad 3 pilots on board Jolly Green. No repeat no major injuries apparent. Corpsman reports student has sprained ankle. Returning to base. Estimated flight time two zero minutes."

The noisy, vibrating chopper rattled over a panorama of the flat, brown Mississippi landscape on the way back. Several years had passed, she knew, since Training Air Wing One had lost one of the reliable T-2s, although a few had limped back with one engine. Had she not reacted to that subtle vibration, the oil-starved engine might have seized catastrophically without warning. Aviators seldom watched oil pressure gauges during high-speed maneuvers. One mistake, or moment of panic, might have found both of them back there in the twisted wreckage.

This escape had given her a whole new life, she thought, a chance which Michael and others never had. Her old life had ended with the dense, oily column of smoke that blackened the sky behind them.

As the helicopter descended slowly toward its large concrete pad at the air station, Allison saw Rusty among the waiting crowd of about a hundred station and squadron people. O'Hara elbowed himself steadily toward the front of the group. The massive rotor blades washed a rippling pattern of air over his flight suit.

Commodore Woodring and the squadron commander, Commander "Stats" Hardin, with Rusty crowded alongside, came up to welcome her safely back. O'Hara would have been chastised for crowding his seniors under any other circumstances, but both knew Rusty and Allison were seeing each other. The commodore appeared mellow about it.

"How do you feel, Allison? You look great," Rusty said. His voice told her he wasn't entirely truthful. "What do you do for an encore?"

"Encore? *Right!* Some people are never satisfied," she said, returning the wisecrack. Despite a shaky voice and weak knees, she shook hands with dozens of smiling shipmates who had crowded the area near the helipad. She'd never realized before how many friends she had. Flight students clustered around Broderick with a raucous, irreverent welcome. He waved off a stretcher and limped with help to the waiting ambulance.

After greeting the well-wishers, Allison felt light perspiration on her face. Rusty's face mirrored concern as he braced his arm firmly around her shoulder and walked her to his car.

"Let's zig by the dispensary before we go to the squadron. The flight surgeon probably wants a look at you. Besides, you must arrive fashionably late for the rest of your adoring fans.''

Her face and hands had turned white. Rusty took her hand and kissed it.

"Okay," she said, her voice weak.

"Chip," the flight surgeon said a few minutes later, "you got off lucky. Most of that bruise should be gone in a week or two." The doctor smiled reassuringly after an examination and a check of her vital signs revealed only a mild case of shock.

"My unofficial prescription," he said, "is a shower and a good night's sleep. My official prescription is that you're off flying for a week."

"Doc, I have too many students and too many hops for that. The other instructors will have to double up to carry my people. How about letting me rope-yarn it for two days, and see how it goes from there?"

Allison knew she wouldn't escape some grounding. But her father had once told her that her great-grandfather had been a horse trader, and maybe she'd inherited some of his bargaining skills.

"Ms. Douglas, the Navy flight program has operated since the 1920s without you. Meridian will not disintegrate overnight if you're grounded for a week."

"Doc, I'm okay, honestly. I have to live with these clowns. Can you imagine what I'd have to put up with if they thought I took time off to nurse a sore bottom? You understand the problem."

She locked her hazel eyes on the flight surgeon as they walked out of the examining room. Rusty stood quietly, far back and out of range.

"Okay, Chip," the doctor said, "two days. But you come back and see me for a preflight checkup before you schedule any training hops. Let me know about any problems in the meantime. I'm not giving you a hard time. My job is to keep good aviators alive.'' He smiled, then turned to scrawl some notes on her chart.

Rusty watched her as they drove from the Naval Dispensary to the TRARON SIX headquarters. She felt the color returning to her cheeks now.

The squadron commander, happy that they'd survived, was content to wait until the following day for details, past her initial report of multiple engine failure. An accident investigation team en route to the smoking wreckage would cordon off the area and begin assessment before darkness made meaningful work impossible.

"How about some dinner tonight, if you're up for that?" Rusty said. He again clasped his arm around her shoulder as they left the headquarters. Color and warmth returned to her hands. She wanted to put her arms around him, close her eyes, and hang on, but this was not the place for that.

"I need to take a shower and get civilized first," she said, running her hands through tousled, matted hair full of Mississippi clay.

Rusty dropped her at the BOQ, hugging her before she went into her room. After she closed the door and leaned against it for a moment, Allison knew she had a lot to live for.

The warm water cascading over her felt reassuring, she thought, even as the large bruise began to throb. As she stood under the soothing shower, she closed her eyes and thought how good it had felt to have Rusty's arms around her this afternoon when she needed it.

The telephone interrupted her thought. She grabbed a towel and dripped barefooted to the phone, rubbing herself dry as she walked.

"Sounds like you had quite an afternoon," Cora Cochrane said. "You must have been really lucky or they'd have kept you overnight at the dispensary, at least."

"Just a black-and-blue butt. The student came away with a sprained ankle. The plane . . . well, that's another story," Allison replied.

"You were lucky, Allison. Both of you."

"I know. I thought about Michael after it happened."

"It's time to put Michael behind you now."

"Funny you should say that. That's what I thought during the ride back in the rescue chopper today. As though I have a whole new life ahead."

"If that's the way you feel, go ahead and live it. But enough of that. I only called to see how you were. You probably have lots to do, and others to call, so I won't keep you."

She must call her father, Allison thought. Otherwise, a TV news report of a Navy trainer crash half a continent away would deeply concern him. In thirty years of flying, she knew Doug never had to punch out. When she called, he tried to appear solicitous but not concerned.

"Dad? It's Allison."

"Hi. The news says y'all lost a T-2 down there today. You're probably calling to tell me it wasn't your airplane and not to worry."

"Well, I'm calling to tell you half of that."

"You mean it *was* yours? You had to punch out today?"

Allison bit her lip, knowing she was about to stretch the truth.

"The ejection wasn't all that bad. My student and I both got out with scratches after a double flameout. You're right though, I didn't want you to worry. I'm okay . . . honest. I'm calling you from the BOQ, not from the hospital. I'm going out on a dinner date tonight."

"Okay, okay, you're tough. But I don't know anyone alive who's punched out of an airplane without it scaring the living daylights out of him. Remember that you're all I've got in this world, Allison. I'm proud of my daughter the naval aviator, but I worry about you too."

"I know, Dad. I'll be careful. I'm all I've got too."

They both laughed.

"Well, okay. Be sure to say hello to my old shipmate Cora Cochrane for me, will you?"

"You betcha, Dad. She's a neat lady."

"Always has been. I love you, daughter."

"I love you too, Dad."

Allison returned to the shower to wash her hair. She felt a strange new thrill at being alive. She had first thought about that when Michael died, but it hadn't hit home until today.

Once out of the shower and dry, she felt suddenly tired, and decided to lie down for a minute before dressing. She wrapped the thick, nappy bathrobe around her, and stretched out on the bed. Soon she was in a dreamless sleep.

Rusty's knock on the door an hour later awakened her. She looked at her watch and, realizing who was there, bolted upright. When she opened the door, half-awake, late-afternoon sunlight poured in behind him, filling the otherwise darkened room. The light made him look more vibrantly alive, more attractive, than ever before. She started to motion him into the room. He drew a dozen red roses from behind his back.

"I'm not quite ready—" she started to say. Rusty set the roses down on the desk nearby, and suddenly closed his arms around her. His lips met hers, and immediately she felt weak again. She didn't want to stop, didn't want to leave his arms now, perhaps never. The door clicked closed, shutting out the world and the blinding sunlight.

"I almost lost you today," he whispered, his lips next to her ear. His warm hands rubbed her back as his arms enfolded her. This was a side of Rusty she hadn't let herself know yet.

"I don't ever want to come that close again."

He must have stared fear in the face long before this, she thought. Rusty knew the emotions she'd felt these last several hours, had probably faced them alone and far away, with no loving arms to hold him, no private place to cry. Her arms tightened around him, her hands against his well-muscled back, as he kissed her again and again.

"Oh, Rusty," she said, and she began to cry. Uncontrolled sobs began to rack her.

He held her head against his chest, her arms still clutching him. Her tears soaked his civilian sport shirt. The only light in the room came through closed venetian blinds, a soft, shadowy light in which they could barely see each other.

"Never again," he murmured. His lips touched the warm, soft side of her neck. A thrill shot through her entire being. She drew him toward her. Her bruise didn't hurt now, or if it did, that didn't matter.

He whispered softly, "I love you, Allison." She'd been given another chance. She knew she must not lose him.

Chapter Eighteen

They'd settled for a quiet dinner at the Meridian Officers' Club that night, with a pillow underneath her seat, and Rusty's hand holding hers beneath the table. She would learn to sleep on her stomach until the bruise healed, Allison thought as she awoke the next morning.

There was no doubt now that she loved Rusty, and that he loved her. In several ways, her world would never be the same again.

Later that morning at the squadron headquarters, the crash site video taken by the preliminary accident investigators sobered her. Closeup images of smoke rose from the unrecognizable, twisted mass of metal which had been her aircraft.

An accident investigation team had flown in from Norfolk, Virginia, early that morning. The investigators' questions were numerous and detailed. Naval aviation pursued accidents with relentless, excruciating investigation, to prevent the same cause from claiming another plane or another pilot. After her interview, they'd quickly ruled out pilot error.

The following day, Allison checked out a T-2 and flew to the operating area where the other aircraft had crashed. She shuddered after making a low pass over burned earth strewn with the charred metal. The ejection had gone so smoothly that neither she nor Broderick fully realized the danger they'd been in until it was over. She turned the aircraft back toward Meridian.

That evening Rusty took her to dinner at Weidman's. Ted and Laramie sat a few tables away. Laramie's tailored red dress showed her figure off to full advantage.

"You had it right," O'Hara said, nodding toward them. Allison thought it strange that Laramie ignored them tonight to the point of rudeness.

"I'm sure they're only discussing today's flying, and he's giving her a little extra help," Allison said with a pseudo-Southern accent. She knew the remark sounded catty.

"Right," Rusty said dryly. "As long as this extra instruction doesn't graduate an aviator who can't aviate." His face became serious again. "Fraternizing with a student isn't kosher either."

"Let's forget about work and just make this an evening for us. That's why we came here, isn't it?" she asked.

"You're right," he replied. "I don't always know when to let go. You keep me on an even keel." Rusty smiled and squeezed her hand again.

When he walked her to the door of her BOQ room later, she slipped her arms around him and kissed him in the dim light. Even now she must be careful, especially now that she loved him and he loved her. They must let nothing spoil it.

A week later, without notice, Laramie Cox filed a sexual harassment complaint letter against Rusty O'Hara with the commanding officer of VT-6. Word shot through the squadron at a speed that only bad news could travel. Allison now understood Laramie's snub at Weidman's.

She waited on the ramp when Rusty returned from a student hop. They sat down at the base snack bar to talk.

"It's a flat-out lie," O'Hara said. "How could she do this?" His face reddened, then his expression turned hard.

"Does she have any grounds at all, any witnesses, anything you may have said?" Allison asked. Her tone showed no doubt of his innocence.

"Nothing. She's got nothing, except that we were alone in the side-by-side T-2 together, and whatever lies she makes up. It's her word against mine. I can't prove a negative any more than she can prove I did anything. Let's get a look at that letter, and quick."

"Why should she do this now? Why not while you were still her instructor? She must know it looks fishy to have waited for several weeks after the alleged offenses."

"We won't know until we read her complaint letter."

"She must be trying to checkmate your flight aptitude report on her, destroy its credibility and yours at the same time."

"She wants you to doubt me too, Allison."

"What do you think?" She looked him in the eye.

O'Hara studied her face. "I think she'll look elsewhere for help."

"Is Ted involved with this?"

"Chadwick's a fool if he is. His precious career, his visions of being an admiral like his daddy, will go down the tubes if he's implicated, and he knows it. By now, Ted wishes he never heard of Laramie Cox. He might even be next on her hit list."

"Rusty, what would you do if you were an attractive female flight student with an aviator father, desperate to get your wings, and knew that you had trouble with at least two instructors?"

"What are you getting at?" O'Hara said.

"Everyone knows who's seeing whom around here. If I downcheck her flying aptitude, it will look as though I'm simply supporting my man."

Rusty nodded. "Wait a minute. You think she's threatening Chadwick by proxy, implying he'll get the same treatment if he doesn't give her an upcheck? Does she really think that will work?"

"Who knows what she thinks, or what *will* work," Allison said. "Whatever happens, this will be nasty. I'm ready to put in the evaluation on her right now. Laramie might pull back if she finds we'll tough it out."

"Or you may get hurt too," he said. "Why should both of us get burned?"

"Rusty, *neither* of us deserves to get burned. Forget the heroics. Laramie would scuttle your career in a minute to get her wings. After lying to smear you, she should lose her commission as well. If we don't stop her now, some unlucky squadron will have a lying, incompetent pilot."

"You don't have much faith in Ted doing the right thing," Rusty said with a wry smile.

"Ted will stand aside and let you take the heat. He and Laramie are two of a kind."

"Okay," Rusty said, "but don't do anything you'll be sorry for later."

"Rusty, Cronin knows we both warned him about her. He got her additional training time and put Ted on as her instructor. He won't perjure himself about our warnings if it comes to a formal investigation."

"Cronin's never flown with her. He's not a firsthand witness to her ineptitude. He can't say anything conclusive one way or the other."

"Wait a minute. Cronin went to the old man based on what we said. The CO authorized the additional hours on Cronin's recommendation. Al's the only one who seems ready to do her any favors. That's a bit strange. Cronin doesn't seem like her type," Allison said.

"You know what?" Rusty said. "I think anyone who will help her get her wings is her type. I told you about her hand-on-my-knee routine. If she thought . . ."

"I don't want to inflate your ego, dear heart," she murmured, squeezing his hand under the table, "but there's a big difference between you and Al Cronin. Why, I could even go for you myself."

"Okay, whatever she said I'll answer with a point-by-point denial. I better see the XO and get a copy of that letter," Rusty said.

She saw hardness in Rusty's usually open face. He would go after Laramie Cox the same way he'd gone after the Iraqi MIGs. Laramie had become the enemy and she had Rusty in her sights, and he didn't like it.

"I'll have my write-up finished up tomorrow," Allison said.

Chapter Nineteen

As Rusty closed the office door and walked toward the Executive Officer a few minutes later, Lieutenant Commander Halvorsen sat with a face that was either sad or angry. Rusty couldn't read the expression.

"Rusty, this is a tough one." He handed a copy of Laramie Cox's typed complaint letter across the desk.

O'Hara read the five pages of narrative, which alleged he had threatened to fail Laramie in aerial tactics if she didn't "cooperate." The paper cited dates, places, late-night phone calls. Laramie had been creative in her writing, persuasive in the theatrics of a victim.

"XO, what's the penalty for a false official statement?" O'Hara asked. One fist tightly gripped the arm of his chair.

"It's a violation of the Uniform Code of Military Justice," Halvorsen answered. "A court-martial offense. A serious charge against an officer, if that's what you mean."

"That's exactly what I mean, XO. This is an official statement, isn't it?" He held up the letter.

"Unless it's withdrawn before an investigation is ordered."

"And you haven't given me an Article 15 warning about self-incrimination."

"This situation hasn't gotten that far yet. I hope it won't. We want to sort out facts right now," Halvorsen said.

"Since you haven't warned me yet, may we talk off the record?"

Halvorsen shifted in his chair. "Okay, Rusty, but make it good."

"Laramie Cox is failing as a jet student. She was failing with me and performed poorly with Allison Douglas on a check-ride. Ask Winslow and you'll find that she's failing with him too. Cronin will confirm that Allison and I warned him about Cox's lack of jet aptitude weeks ago. The CO approved extra flying hours for her, which did no good. All that's history."

"What does her flying ability have to do with harassment allegations?" Halvorsen's face showed he didn't understand.

"Harassment isn't Cox's real agenda, XO. Getting wings, at any cost, is her objective. She can't handle jets. I'm writing a flight aptitude report which recommends she be dropped."

Rusty paused for a few seconds to let the words sink in, then continued.

"Take her up yourself, have the CO take her up. Have *any* instructor in the squadron take her up. Don't take my word for it!"

"Rusty, you haven't made the connection between this and the harassment complaint," Halvorsen said.

"This is her red herring to checkmate being bilged out, XO. Undermine the report-writer and you cast doubt on the report. There's nothing to answer. I haven't done any of this. She can't *prove* allegation one, not even close. Laramie has no witnesses, no substantiation, nothing. If this were true, she would have reported it to the Naval Investigative Service. They'd have tapped her phone. She didn't do that, because there were no phone calls. Laramie is no great pilot, but she's cunning. The woman's blowing smoke, XO."

"She claims you fondled her in the aircraft, had your hands all over her while you were flying. How do you disprove that?"

"The question is how does she prove it? Why didn't she

report allegations like that weeks ago? What made her wait until now? The answer is that it didn't happen. I'll take a lie-detector test to clear this nonsense up. I also expect her to take one. That should settle it, wouldn't you say?''

"Lie-detector tests aren't admissible in many legal proceedings. By the way, what about Chip Douglas? You mentioned she also had Cox up for a check-ride."

"Yes.'' Rusty had hoped to keep Allison out of this.

"Will Chip confirm your claims before an investigation board about Cox's flying ability? Your evaluation might sound like sour grapes after her complaint."

"Any instructor you put in an airplane with Laramie Cox will tell you the same thing. That includes Chadwick."

"I'll talk to the CO, Rusty. This will become dynamite if the case goes public. We'll have to be painfully thorough."

"What happens when Ensign Cox can't prove her allegations? Does that make a case for a false official statement? Anyone who makes vicious accusations deserves to be accountable if she can't prove them. She needs to take the heat as well as dish it out."

"That's a whole 'nother issue, Rusty," Halvorsen said.

"And Laramie Cox's flying ability? I suppose that's a whole 'nother issue too?"

"That will get a thorough scrub no matter what happens. Cox has drawn attention to herself. She'll have to back up whatever she says, as you will. You know the system is basically fair."

"No one can prove something that didn't happen, XO, and that's what this is, a zero. There's nothing to prove."

"Nonetheless, Rusty, there is due process required by regulations."

"Perhaps Cox is betting that the Navy will shut her up and give her the wings, avoid another high-profile harassment case in the media at any cost," O'Hara said.

"What would you say, Rusty?"

"I'll bet she walks out of here without them. In fact, if

the Navy wants to give her wings, they can give her mine. I won't need them anymore.''

The XO took a deep breath. His face turned from serious to sad.

"Rusty," Halvorsen said quietly, "don't do anything rash."

At dinner that night, O'Hara described the interview with Halvorsen. Allison read and reread the letter intently.

"Rusty, we were together those evenings she says she received phone calls. I'll tell Halvorsen that, make a sworn statement, whatever they want. The woman's a vicious liar."

"That will only draw you into this mess. Laramie will say your evaluation backs up mine, because of our relationship. Some people will believe that, regardless of the truth. Better if you don't even turn in your report. Please stay out of this and let me handle it."

"Rusty, you're a bullheaded fool!" Allison's eyes blazed. She almost shouted at him. "That little witch will lie, cheat, steal, maybe even kill to get those wings. Laramie doesn't care who gets hurt."

"I can beat her; I can beat this. She's flat lying and she can't prove a word of it!"

"Laramie will cry to an investigating board that you're the big, bad, predatory fighter pilot and she's the innocent, dewy-eyed student. She'll have you hog-tied and butchered like a Montana steer when she's through. You've got to let me, and others, help you now."

"Allison, I don't want you dragged into this thing. I can handle her, believe me." He put his arms around her. "Allison, I love you and I don't want anything to hurt you."

"Hurt me? What could hurt me more than to see you ruined by some lying excuse for a woman? I'll see Halvorsen tomorrow and tell him that I was with you every one of those evenings she alleges the phone calls were made."

"That will create a lot of false rumors about us, you know," Rusty said.

"Who cares what they think? We have nothing to hide. No guts, no Air Medal, as you fighter pilots say. I'm also going to have a little set-to with Ms. Ensign Cox, woman to woman."

"That's not a good idea. What do you expect to accomplish, Allison?"

"Laramie Cox thinks she's going to buffalo the Navy, you, me, all of us. She's not that smart. Nobody's bigger or tougher than the service, and certainly not that little . . . shrew." Allison hesitated for a moment. "Or maybe I'll just tear out all her hair in a cat fight." They both laughed.

"Okay, okay. I still think it's a bad idea for you to get involved. But if you have to, talk to Halvorsen first," Rusty said. "Then decide what to do with Laramie. Don't give her anything to use against you."

"Wouldn't it be nice to talk about something else?" She moved closer to Rusty and began to rub his shoulders.

Chapter Twenty

Allison hadn't expected much from her half-hour with the executive officer of VT-6. Lieutenant Commander Halvorsen was among those unconvinced that women belonged in naval aviation. Laramie Cox had brought him an embarrassing problem. And Allison had recently lost the first squadron aircraft in years during a still-unresolved aircraft accident.

"Okay, Chip," Halvorsen said, "so Laramie Cox isn't another Amelia Earhart. How does that square with her allegation that Rusty was harassing her?"

Had she been a male officer, she thought, the XO's words would have been more blunt. "Her thinking's pretty transparent to me," Allison replied. "Undermine the flight aptitude process by attacking the evaluators. Perhaps she's betting that we'll avoid another so-called scandal by letting her slide by. It's a clever ploy, but desperate."

"If you're right, she'll also have to discredit you. She can't get only Rusty written off and expect to survive."

"Easy. She'll allege conspiracy because Rusty and I see each other. Maybe she hopes I'll believe her story and turn on Rusty. Who knows what she thinks? The bottom line, XO, is that Laramie Cox is a potential disaster in jets. Don't take my word for that. Take her up yourself. On second thought, be careful. She might accuse you of sexual harassment."

Allison knew she'd missed a good opportunity to keep

her mouth shut. "I'm probably the only one around here who's safe from that allegation," she said.

"Okay, I hear you," Halvorsen said.

The XO might still be unsure about her motives. On the other hand, the situation was a Gordian knot. COs and XOs earned a year's pay for decisions on issues like this. One day, she expected to be in Halvorsen's shoes as a squadron XO. She didn't envy him now.

Later that day, Allison searched out Laramie. The flight schedule revealed that she had a training flight with Ted that afternoon.

Allison found her in the hangar and walked up on her blind side while she spoke to three of the other students.

"Do you have a minute, Laramie?"

Laramie didn't quite wheel around, but Allison's presence seemed no surprise to her.

"Fire away," she said.

"I'd like a word with you privately, when you're finished. There's no hurry."

"Anything you have to say to me, you can say in front of my friends, Lieutenant."

Embarrassed shock flashed across the students' faces. Everyone knew about the letter, and about Allison and Rusty. Laramie's answer, however, rode the thin edge of insubordination.

"I'm in no hurry," Allison repeated, ignoring Laramie's comment.

Allison stood motionless, her expression unchanged. In less than a minute the other students found reasons to be elsewhere. The two women stood alone in the corner of the hangar.

"Word's going around that Rusty O'Hara's been harassing you with threats and obscene phone calls," Allison said. Her blunt approach was calculated.

"He wanted me to pay too high a price for my wings. I wouldn't do that."

"Just what price is that?"

"Surely I don't have to draw diagrams for you, Lieutenant Douglas. When I wouldn't 'cooperate,' he marked me down on flight aptitude. Worry about his advances affected my flight performance. I was nervous every time I flew with him." Laramie fumbled with her hands.

"Laramie, your jet tactics were lousy on our check-ride. I hope I didn't make you nervous also."

"You're Rusty O'Hara's girlfriend. You'd do anything to protect him." A sharp edge crept into the blond's voice.

"Not if Rusty tried to two-time me," Allison shot back. "That would make me angry, even vengeful. Convince me that Rusty was harassing female pilots, and I'll step up and help you nail him. Show me as you would an investigation board and you'll have a full-bore supporter."

"Lieutenant O'Hara's very aggressive in the side-by-side T-2s," Laramie said. "It's difficult to concentrate on flying when someone fondles you at ten thousand feet." Laramie paused briefly. "You mean he never came on to you like that?"

Laramie hadn't spent all of her teen years roping steers, Allison thought. "No, but I've read your letter. Your accusations are both specific and deadly. If he did what you said, I want him stopped as much as you do."

Allison wondered if Ted had put her up to the letter. "Sexual harassment has happened before in the Navy," she said, "and maybe in flight training. If so, now is the time to stop it. That means proof. Find another woman who'll support what you say and testify against Rusty, and you'll have my full cooperation. My help would be welcome, wouldn't it?" Laramie had ignored her offer the first time.

"I don't know if anyone else has had problems with him, and I don't care. That's not the point. I *have*."

Laramie appeared to be testing a programmed argument. Her acting ability seemed impressive.

"Sure, imagine that," Allison said. "Imagine too that he's been here for almost a year and has trained several other women students. Up to now no one else has complained. . . ."

"Several of his women students have failed. That doesn't mean that the others haven't 'cooperated' in order to pass."

"Some of Rusty's male students have also failed. So have several of mine. This is a tough program. People who don't make it through are not bad people."

"Getting my wings means more to me than some people think." Laramie's voice showed a nervous edge now.

"To make your allegations stick, you need more than your word against his. The outcome is important for every woman in naval aviation, not just you, Laramie. If you lose, every woman aviator looks bad."

"I'm only an ensign, Lieutenant Douglas. This big-picture stuff is not my job. I'm trying to get my wings, and fight my way out of an intolerable situation."

Laramie had worked on this argument for a while, perhaps with help, Allison thought. "Keep in mind the seriousness of a false official statement if your allegations don't prove out."

"Is that some kind of threat, Lieutenant?"

"No, that's a fact. There's a difference. Women get no free lunches in naval aviation, no more right than men to make unproven charges. We must perform better than men simply to come out even. Your flying record won't make a predominantly male board totally sympathetic."

"If the Navy can't settle this sensibly, the media and the Armed Services Committee will. The world outside the Navy will keep this in perspective."

Bingo, thought Allison. "You have more confidence in that crowd than I do. Because the media covers your story doesn't mean they're your friend. Investigative reporters trace your life back to the day you were born, interview every man you've ever dated. If you have any skeletons in your closet, they'll parade them in front of the world. When the press learns you're using them and exerting political influence, both they and the congressionals will turn on you like a copperhead."

"Lieutenant, that sounds like another threat," Cox said.

"Facts are not threats, Laramie. Unless you don't have your facts straight." Allison shrugged, and turned toward her again. "But we're in the real world. I sure hope your evidence extends beyond your word against his. As the accuser, you have the burden of proof."

"The phone company can provide records of the calls. That will prove it." Laramie turned and began to pace.

"Come off it, Ms. Cox! Unless the calls were long distance, you know there's no record. If they were direct-dialed on the station's internal exchange, there's definitely nothing. Even if the calls could be documented, that wouldn't prove that Rusty said anything wrong, unless you had someone else listening in who could testify. Your other alternative would have been to tape the calls, of course."

Allison paused and closed the distance between herself and Laramie. Working hours had ended. The hangar was deserted now.

"It's a violation of federal law to record phone conversations without notifying the other person. Even if you had such evidence, that would make the tapes inadmissible as evidence. But you needn't worry about that, because you don't have any."

"What are you trying to say, Lieutenant Douglas?" Laramie's face had turned red, her expression changed. The confident look was gone.

"Someone might ask why you didn't report your charges more promptly, either to the command or the Naval Criminal Investigative Service. NIS could have obtained a warrant, tapped your phone legally, provided proof. You might think about what you've started by submitting this letter. You could find yourself in more trouble than you can handle. False official statements are a court-martial offense."

Laramie's eyes scanned the area. Perhaps she looked to see if anyone could overhear their conversation, Allison thought. The student would characterize Allison's words as attempted intimidation if an investigation followed.

"I'm ready for trouble. I have nothing to lose," Laramie replied.

Allison silently had to agree.

Chapter Twenty-one

Ted Chadwick knew he had a problem. As Laramie Cox talked to him as he prepared a candlelight dinner in his apartment, he thought of her charges against O'Hara. Chadwick couldn't believe that she had been dumb enough to do that, or that he'd been foolish enough to associate with her. Assuring Laramie that she'd pass aerial tactics had been rash, now that he had flown with her. His hormones had overruled his brain.

Perhaps she'd attacked O'Hara to destroy the credibility of a report from which she expected the worst. If Chadwick couldn't talk her out of this, she would inexorably drag him into this cesspool.

"Ted, you certainly are a clever man," she said. Perhaps she wanted reassurance of his support, now that the going had become tough.

"And you, dear Laramie, are the most gorgeous woman aviator alive," he whispered. Flattery always pleased her greatly.

Now was not the time to convince her to withdraw the troublesome letter against O'Hara, Chadwick thought.

He opened a large bottle of pouilly-fuissé for them in his gourmet kitchen. Laramie, he'd learned, was accustomed to the finer things. Perhaps later, after dinner with some good wine, she would look at things less emotionally. Ensuring that she was in a good mood was very important. Now she appeared distracted about something.

"Ted, will you back me up as you said, tell them that I can handle jet tactics, that I'll pass?"

"Of course, Laramie." Chadwick saw a sudden opening. "I wouldn't have done what you did about Rusty O'Hara, though. You should have talked to me about that first."

He tossed the salad lightly and shook out the excess water. Chadwick was furious at her, but he'd gain nothing by showing that. "The letter was overkill. It'll come back to bite you if you can't prove what you've alleged."

"What I said in the letter is true. Why withdraw it? Besides, the letter's in, and that's that." She shrugged.

Laramie's lying, Chadwick thought. She would have told him about O'Hara before she wrote the letter. The woman couldn't prove a thing. His father would be furious if Ted besmirched the family name and his career over this silly student. The old man had warned him about women before this one.

"Why not call O'Hara?" Ted said. "Tell him you'll withdraw the letter if he'll be reasonable, give you the benefit of the doubt, however you want to word it. If he'll do that, Allison will surely go along. Neither of them want the trouble that will come with that letter . . . and you don't either."

"Do you think that would work? O'Hara is fanatical about flight standards."

"He also knows that you've tagged him with the kiss of death. If he can't clear himself, he's finished, DFC or no DFC."

"Maybe I should let him worry for a few more days. That might soften him up more."

"No. By then the system will order an investigation, a formal inquiry. Once that happens, you no longer control the situation and couldn't stop it if you wanted to. An investigation takes on a life of its own."

Ted refilled her empty wineglass.

"Make a preemptive strike now," he said. "Withdraw

the letter tomorrow if O'Hara says anything encouraging when you call him. That makes you look decisive.''

"That makes me look like a fool!''

"You'll look reasonable, in Rusty's eyes. It defuses the situation for both of you. You'll motivate him to do the right thing, which he certainly doesn't feel like now. You won't have to prove anything. Your options are open to resubmit the charges later if O'Hara doesn't do what you want. The advantages and control are on your side.''

Chadwick paused to let the logic soak in.

"Unless you can prove your charges and get someone else who will testify against O'Hara,'' he continued, "this will backfire.''

Laramie remembered Allison's offer to help her if another woman would testify, but no one else had. For good reason. Allison probably knew that. She also remembered the flight instructor's comment about the seriousness of a false official statement.

Laramie now understood that she'd unleashed a monster that could turn and eat her alive. Ted and Allison had reached similar conclusions. Perhaps she had miscalculated. Flight training was different from life on the ranch, where owning land as far as you could see gave a sense of power over events.

"Okay, I see the politics of this,'' she said. "Whether I'm right or wrong doesn't matter. Making waves can do nothing but hurt me. I'll call O'Hara now.'' Laramie walked to the telephone directory, wrote down Rusty's number, and dialed.

Chadwick decided to let her, before she changed her mind. He hoped she didn't mess up the phone call.

"O'Hara,'' Rusty answered after two rings.

"Lieutenant O'Hara, this is Laramie Cox. I need to talk to you.''

Rusty's initial reaction was to slam down the phone, his second to tell her what she could do with her letter, and where she could go. His hand trembled. He decided not to do either, but silently signaled Allison to the phone to listen. He scrawled *Laramie* on a slip of paper and watched her eyes go wide.

"Okay, Laramie, it's your quarter."

"You're not recording this conversation, are you?"

"That's illegal. To answer your question, no, I'm not."

"I've rethought the letter and want to withdraw it. I don't want to hurt you or your career, but I need your assurance that you'll be fair to me."

Rusty's face has turned deep red, his hand now clenched into a white-knuckled fist. No time now for temper. He'd better play this game gently or lose it.

"It's hard to answer that. You know that letter was a total pack of lies. None of what you alleged happened, not a bit of it. Now you're asking *me* to be fair?"

"Okay, I was wrong. I was desperate to get my wings, to pass. My father was an aviator during Vietnam. How can I go home and face him if I fail out of flight school? I apologize, and I want to make things right. I don't want to fly jets, or fighters, or anything like that. I just don't want to be disenrolled." Her voice sounded as though she was about to cry.

Rusty had used the moments of her conversation to decide. Neither he nor the Navy tolerated officers who lied. This, however, was no time to foreclose options.

"I promise you that I will think very carefully about it, and do the right thing. That's all I can say now."

Perhaps she'd hoped for more, but at least it wasn't an irate, flat turndown. Maybe his veiled language implied he would make a deal. To recall the charges would be embarrassing, but she could do it, he thought, although she'd better waste no time.

"All right," she said, "I'll withdraw the letter tomorrow. I'm depending on your good faith. Good night, and thank you."

Rusty sat quietly for a moment. Allison's warmth remained next to him after he hung up the phone.

"Can you believe that?"

He stood and walked across the room, then paced back. His face remained red; his hands opened and closed into fists again. His lips formed ugly words Allison could read easily.

She watched him silently. He paced some more. The anger soon drained from his face.

"I'm not going to change the report, you know," he said. "I promised her I would do the right thing, and I will—the right thing for the Navy, and ultimately for her. She's not even smart enough to know that being sent home might save her life."

Allison went over and put her arms around him.

"You're a good man, Rusty, a very good man," she whispered, and kissed him.

Chapter Twenty-two

"How did you ever do it, Rusty?" Halvorsen's face combined amazement and relief when he told O'Hara that Laramie had withdrawn her letter.

"I didn't do anything, XO. She called me. I told her that she knew the letter was a pack of lies. At the end, she said she'd pull it."

Halvorsen got up from behind his desk and walked around toward Rusty. "You still have some flight evaluation reports on her that you haven't turned in yet."

"XO, I apologize. You know how I love paperwork. You'll have them by Friday . . . so you can read them before you go to the officers' club."

Allison's report on Laramie Cox's flight with her was already complete. While her narrative carefully detailed Laramie's inability, it reflected only one hop. Rusty had the tough job, numerous hours of instruction over several weeks. Fortunately, she knew he'd kept good records. As they sat in his BOQ room, Rusty pounded out a draft on her portable typewriter with two fingers. Allison knew his recommendation wasn't in doubt.

"What do you think Chadwick will do when these reports hit the front office?" Rusty asked. "And what will Cronin say? He knows better than to ask me to change this, even if he were so inclined."

"She's pathetic, Rusty. If she's not simply lying again,

about her father being an aviator in Vietnam, your phone conversation with her explains some things.''

"Pathetic, sure she's pathetic—incompetent, conniving. Worse, she's a naval officer who lies. She'd ruin someone's career, manipulate and threaten, undermine a system built on integrity, all to accommodate herself. I wouldn't live with that even if she were God's gift to naval aviation. It's pretty simple. Either she goes—or I do.''

"Rusty, you can't be serious.''

"Listen, if our system can't wash out a student with flight ineptitude and moral turpitude, I've picked the wrong place to work.''

Rusty looked sad now.

"Don't make this so confrontational. She may be bad news, but she's not an enemy MIG,'' she said.

"She's *more* dangerous than an enemy MIG. You know what to expect from those guys. You don't worry about them killing our own flight deck people if they make a bad carrier landing.''

"The system has washed out students ever since it started. We've both let our share of them go,'' Allison said.

"Some are more politically sensitive than others,'' Rusty replied, his voice full of revulsion.

"Politics won't win this one. I'm sure of it,'' she said. Allison put her arms around him. "Once you finish that report, we'll go get ourselves a nice dinner.''

"Great!'' He smiled broadly. "I'll hurry this up.''

Cronin sat with the CO and XO in the CO's office. They examined the two flight aptitude reports on Laramie. Nothing in her flight record showed either report to be an aberration.

"The extra flying hours didn't do Ms. Cox any good, Al,'' the CO said. "Nice try, but no cigar for her.''

"We had to give her a fair chance, and she's had one. We're clean on proceeding with a washout on her,'' Cronin said.

Laramie had avoided Cronin lately. He knew of her involvement with Chadwick. She and Ted deserved each other. Cronin considered Chadwick to be a smooth-talking, snooty admiral's son.

"XO," the CO said, "have Chadwick write an evaluation on her. He's had her long enough."

True, Cronin thought.

"Good idea, Al," the CO said.

"Sir?"

"Giving Ensign Cox flying hours with more than one instructor, especially with her letter about Rusty O'Hara, might have been even better if she'd had more time with Allison Douglas."

Chadwick decided not to tell Laramie that he'd been ordered to write an evaluation. That would buy another week or more of peace and quiet, give her less time to react. The XO wouldn't let him read the other two reports, but he could guess what at least one of them said. O'Hara's report didn't matter to him, nor did Allison's. His own evaluation must ensure there was no mud on his flight suit when this was over.

"I'm not sure I did the right thing in pulling the letter," Laramie said to Chadwick later after dinner at his place.

"Sure you did." Chadwick put his arm around her. "To withdraw that letter was the smartest thing you could do, especially if witnesses and proof couldn't confirm what you say. No doubt Rusty will get away with murder, but that's better than you getting in trouble."

"You don't have any doubt that it all happened, do you, Ted?"

"If you say it happened, it happened. That's not the point. Never fight a battle you can't win. You end up getting bloody unnecessarily and the final result is the same. Always exit losing situations as early and gracefully as possible."

"You're saying take the easy way out, Ted."

"I'm saying take the *smart* way out, where you lose the least, retreat without public embarrassment, and live to fight another day. If they decided against you, then pursued charges of a false official statement, you'd be in much more serious trouble."

"But you said you believed me!"

"What I believe doesn't matter. It's what the system believes, and what they do about it. Do you really think a board of male pilots who drink with Rusty O'Hara will nail the old war hero on the undocumented word of a woman student? Don't second-guess your action now. You did the right thing, the smart thing."

Laramie pulled her arms more closely around Ted. She liked to hear that. She needed support now, and he was all she had. Well, she thought, not quite.

Chapter Twenty-three

"Rusty, come quick. Listen to this!" Allison yelled. She leaped out of her seat and turned up the volume on the TV in her BOQ room.

"Hallelujah!" she shouted, and clasped her arms around a surprised O'Hara. She pointed to the screen and started to wheel him around as though doing a jig.

"Incredible! One day the Defense Department says women can't fly combat aircraft, the next they knock down every obstacle. The news says Navy and Air Force women will join combat squadrons within a few months. Even the Marines, with no women aviators now, have to train some. This is almost *too* good. I wonder who'll try to stop it before it happens."

"Hey, don't go borrowing trouble," Rusty said. "Your glass is more than half-full already."

Little warning had preceded the sweeping policy change, she thought. To avoid false hopes, Allison hadn't attached much importance to recent media speculation that this might happen.

Now she understood the instant euphoria of a lottery winner. This day had flavored her dreams since the evening at NAS Norfolk when she was ten. Hundreds of other women must feel the same way now, she thought.

The tough, long, scary days had been worth it. Women would now be full members of the exclusive club which had previously excluded them from its most vital work.

She hoped merit and not politics drove the decision. Politics and landing aboard a carrier in the blackness of a stormy, moonless night were incompatible. Neither politicians nor assertive feminists could will that to happen.

Time to celebrate, and to share the wonder of this news with the man she loved.

"Come here," she said as she reached out her arms. "I want to borrow some trouble." She drew Rusty closer and kissed him, again and again.

"I'm very happy for you," he whispered, holding her close.

They could be in the same fleet squadron now, Rusty thought, perhaps deploy on the same carrier. Too much to ask for, he thought. Would they ever find privacy aboard ship? Ingenuity would prevail. Why worry about that now?

Her warmth and subtle fragrance still overwhelmed him. Despite his optimism, Rusty saw a dark side. Eventually they'd be separated. Even marriage could only reduce that possibility, he thought, not eliminate it. The Navy would retain its policy of keeping couples together when possible.

But sooner or later, though, the "needs of the service," the circumstance to which all service members must yield, would disrupt their lives together. Separation never bothered him before. There'd been no loved one important enough before Allison.

The two flight aptitude reports on Laramie Cox had clearly been written by separate instructors without collaboration, "Stats" Hardin thought as he reread the documents in his office at Training Squadron Six. The deficiencies they revealed were remarkably similar.

O'Hara's report was terse and precise, detailing the woman's performance in each aspect of the tactical curriculum. The report summarized:

Despite ten hours of additional instruction, ENS Cox consistently fails to maintain affirmative control of jet trainer aircraft during high-speed aerial maneuvers. She also fails to make timely final approach corrections during landings ashore. This deficiency makes questionable her ability to land aboard ship, even in ideal weather and sea state conditions. ENS Cox is dangerously unequipped for foul-weather landings, at sea or ashore. Any attempt to land without supervision would jeopardize her life, the safety of her aircraft, and the lives of flight deck crewmembers.

Hardin read further down, to the section marked "Recommendation." He knew what it would say.

Board action to disenroll ENS Cox for inadequate aptitude for flight.

O'Hara's document was devoid of speculation or conjecture. He expected the report to receive intense scrutiny, after Laramie's allegations against him.

Hardin turned to Allison's report. Her document was a conversational narrative which examined Laramie's deficiencies thoroughly. Less harsh than O'Hara's, it touched the same weak points and cited examples. She must have expected to defend it like a doctoral thesis, Hardin thought. He read the neatly typed report:

ENS Cox has tried valiantly but without success to master the skills of tactical jet aviation. Inadequate eye-hand coordination in full-power landings poses a safety of flight hazard to herself and to others. She unfortunately lacks both confidence and competence in aerial flight in the jet environment. ENS Cox is not ready for carrier qualification now, nor have addi-

tional training hours produced any progress toward that end.

Hardin again read the "Recommendation" section, again assessing its net effect in advance.

> *ENS Cox is regrettably recommended for disenrollment from the flight program for inadequate aptitude. This recommendation considers the mortal danger to herself and others, and her inability to meet minimum standards for jet aircraft maneuver required at sea.*

Nicely worded but deadly, he thought. Only Ted Chadwick's remained to be included before the formal disenrollment process began. He expected no surprises.

Word had circulated, probably by Laramie herself, that her father knew people in Washington. Hardin expected he and the commodore would feel the heat if that were true. Halvorsen told him Rusty had threatened to turn in his wings if Cox passed. If he and Giles Woodring had the courage they were paid for, Hardin thought, that wouldn't happen.

Captain Giles Woodring, COMTRAWING ONE, walked back and forth in his office the following day, deep in thought. High overcast lent grayness to the light pouring through the blinds into his wood-paneled office. He'd almost completed his tour of duty as top man at Meridian. The assignment prepared him for selection to rear admiral when the next board met in nine months. For twenty-five years he'd flown the Navy's aircraft, commanded squadrons and an air group aboard ship, and now the training wing. Three times he had ejected from flak-ridden or engine-dead planes; once he'd spent two days in a rubber raft in the Mediterranean. Only luck and an A-6 Intruder attack bomber which had absorbed more than its share of anti-aircraft shell fragments had kept him from becoming a long-term guest in the Hanoi Hilton.

Woodring pulled the Naval Criminal Investigative Service folder from his desk drawer. His brows knitted. Commander Hardin wisely called in NIS when Cox submitted her complaint letter against O'Hara, he thought. Even though she withdrew the document a few days later, NIS Agent Antonio Cervera had time to learn some interesting things. Cervera's conclusions weren't surprising. Shocking, but not surprising. The surprises for several people, he thought, were yet to come.

Cora answered the telephone in Woodring's anteroom. Her friend Sophie in Admiral Chadwick's Pentagon office was on the other end.

"The old man's cranked up this morning about some female flight student named Cox," the other chief said.

Cora winced. "Thanks for the heads-up. Let me get him on the line," she said as she pushed the hold button.

"Commodore, it's Admiral Chadwick's office. His writer says it's about the Cox case. Shall I stall him for a minute or so?"

"No, Chief, I'm ready for the . . . admiral. Put him on."

The phone clicked again.

"Good morning, Commodore," Admiral Chadwick said. "I have a sensitive one for you. You have an advanced flight student, an Ensign Laramie Cox. She's having trouble with an instructor named O'Hara who is sexually harassing her. I want to—"

"Admiral, I'm familiar with the case." Giles Woodring knew that he'd interrupted a senior aviator who might sit on his selection board. What, he wondered, had Laramie done now?

"Ensign Cox withdrew her accusations against Lieutenant O'Hara before we opened a formal investigation. There's real question about whether she told the truth. I have a recommendation that we charge her with making a false official statement. Two flight aptitude reports I received this morning indicate she's failing jet tactics—''

"You don't seem to understand," Admiral Chadwick said. "I had a call from the Hill. Her father was an A-4 driver who flew strikes from USS *Midway* during Vietnam. He's tight with the Montana delegation and elsewhere. Montana people sit on the Senate Appropriations and House Armed Services Committees, as you recall. Her father believes she's being shafted by the training command because she's a woman."

"With all due respect to her father, Admiral, that's horse-hockey. Laramie Cox shows a classic failing flight student profile. She was okay in props, but can't handle jets. The woman's had three instructors here. The first is the only lieutenant I have with a DFC from the Gulf War. The second is the smartest woman aviator on the station, a former flag pilot. You already know her present instructor."

"No, who is that?"

"Your son, Ted, sir."

Giles Woodring heard a deep breath on the other end.

"What possibilities can we discuss?"

You swine, Woodring thought.

"The system isn't the problem. She's failed jet tactics badly so far. Two flight aptitude reports I hold recommend her disenrollment. An additional ten hours of flight instruction hasn't helped, but it answers the mail about short shrift or discrimination. Since her father's an aviator, he knows she can't attempt carrier landings without mortal risk if she can't handle tactics. I'd rather send her home as a washout now than in a box later. If she kills herself in a Navy airplane, and we didn't disenroll her when we should, her father would have *real* reason to beat up on us."

"And O'Hara?"

"NIS investigated that. The allegations against him are groundless. In fact, Ms. Cox may be in more trouble than a simple flight training failure. Several people here may be involved in conduct unbecoming. This will be messy if it goes sour.''

Chadwick wanted a quick fix, Woodring thought—the right answer to soothe Capitol Hill. There was no right answer. Worse, his son was in the middle. Ted would have to write a flight aptitude evaluation on Laramie. Old Chadwick must wonder whether Ted had poached on the hapless student yet.

"Giles, I appreciate your candid input. While not encouraging, it does help. I'll get back to you." Chadwick hung up the phone without waiting for Woodring's response.

The old man really had himself in a bind, and so did his dear boy, Woodring thought. Either would sacrifice Woodring in a heartbeat to avoid blame.

Too bad for them. Woodring had cheated death several times. He enjoyed the luxury of doing the right thing, and paying for it in full, if necessary. He returned to reading Cervera's NIS file. Good thing Laramie had submitted the complaint letter against O'Hara. Otherwise he wouldn't have learned so many interesting things.

Chapter Twenty-four

Three days later, Halvorsen summoned Rusty again. When O'Hara arrived from the flight line, he knew his face must have a wary look.

"Relax, Rusty. This has nothing to do with Laramie Cox. It's good news."

He'd make up his own mind about good news, O'Hara thought. That had become relative lately. Halvorsen handed him an incoming naval message from the chief of naval personnel. Rusty's name, highlighted in flourescent yellow, jumped off the page. The list of officers selected for the Naval Test Pilot School at NAS Patuxent River, Maryland, carried only one name from Meridian.

Rusty had applied for test pilot school soon after arriving at Meridian, before he met Allison. After combat in the Navy's most sophisticated aircraft, test flying was the ultimate professional adventure, and the most career-enhancing.

Two months ago, this news would have produced a whoop of joy. Now it meant he'd transfer in six months or less, and would have to leave Allison behind. She had yet to decide about her own career objectives. Everything had happened so fast.

"Thanks, XO. Thoughtful of you to let me know right away. I've hoped for test pilot school ever since I left the fleet. No offense to the flight instruction business, but this is—"

"I know, Rusty. Wouldn't mind being on that list myself," the XO said.

As Rusty walked out into the afternoon sunlight, he chuckled at the irony. The woman he loved wanted to fly fighters with the fleet, and now she could. He had wanted to be a test pilot, and now he could do that. These great career victories were no longer unqualified joys. Something had to give in each of their lives.

Allison would return from her training hop in an hour. That gave him time to think, but not enough. Before he had decided how to break the news, her white and orange T2-C trainer taxied up near base operations. After she'd sent her student off, she and Rusty went around the corner of the building to be alone.

"Rusty, that's terrific news!" she said when he told her, hugging him so tight he thought his ribs would crack. "You're a very lucky man."

"I already know that, but it has nothing to do with test pilot school." He wrapped his arms around her and closed his eyes.

"In six months or less, I'll ship out for Pax River."

"I know," she said, resting her head on his shoulder. "This is important for you. We'll find a way to live with it. I'd like test pilot school one day too. My last boss recommended me."

Whatever way they found would be difficult, he thought.

"Maybe you can get an East Coast billet, Norfolk or Oceana," he said. "Perhaps apply for the RAG in Norfolk. That's only a short hop to Norfolk from Pax River. We'd be together on weekends. There may be some fleet-related flying jobs at Pax, who knows?"

The Replacement Air Group, or RAG, schooled fleet pilots in first-line combat aircraft, training Allison would need to fly the F-14 or F-18 at sea. He knew she could easily end up somewhere else.

If he were Ted Chadwick, Rusty thought, his father could arrange her transfer anywhere. That wouldn't happen. Allison had chosen him, Rusty the unconnected, Rusty the uninfluential, Rusty the unpolitical. He had no "rabbi," as Navy people called influential mentors. At least not yet. She'd have to fend for herself too. Allison's only heavy-hitter was the three-star former boss from San Diego who'd recommended her for test pilot school. The admiral might help, but Allison wouldn't pull strings.

"Allison, will you marry me?" he said.

She hugged him closer.

"You know I would. This may not be the time, though. We have so many things to work out."

"Test pilot school isn't everything in the world. . . ."

"If you're thinking about turning down NTPS to stay here with me, that's gallant, but unwise. You'll never have another chance. I want to go through the RAG, get into a fleet squadron, and prove that I can fly F-14s as well as anybody. Maybe someday I'll get NTPS too. I drafted the letter requesting transfer to the RAG the day after the Defense announcement came out. . . ."

"Then why not send it in?"

"The same reason you hesitated about test pilot school. We were born to accomplish certain things, or die trying. I know what this school means to you. I know what you mean to me. No way is balancing this going to be easy."

"And I used to think dogfighting with Iraqi MIGs was hairy," he said. "But if our future is meant to be, we'll make it work."

"For one of us to give up a career or an opportunity like test pilot school would be easy," she said, "but it wouldn't be right. You've landed TPS. We don't know whether I'll get a fleet seat, or when. It's too early to foreclose options."

"Send in that letter," he said. "You won't be happy until you do.

"Come over here and talk to me," he said, extending his hand to her. "I feel lucky."

Chapter Twenty-five

A few days after the test pilot selection list came out, the phone rang in the squadron office for Rusty. The aviation assignments detailer in Washington was on the line.

"Hey, Rusty," his Gulf War shipmate said. "I have good news for you." O'Hara remained wary.

"Okay, Jake, what are you forked-tongue snake-oil salesmen peddling this week?"

"A sudden vacancy popped up in the test pilot class convening week after next. The selectee got crunched in an auto accident. He won't fly anything for a while. Since you're a bachelor and an easy, quick move, I want to plug you into that seat. That gives you a head start. The others on your list won't start until next fiscal year."

His buddy genuinely wanted to help him, and solve his own urgent problem. Jake, he thought, didn't know about Allison.

"Jake, can I call you back tomorrow?"

"Okay, Rusty, but no later. I have to fill that seat ASAP or the admiral will be on my case."

"Roger, Jake. Tomorrow for sure."

Rusty put down the phone slowly. If he turned Jake down, he could forestall or postpone the inevitable separation from Allison. The sword had hung over them since the list came out. After his urging, she submitted the letter request for a RAG assignment followed by a fleet squadron. Months could pass before she knew anything. Or, like himself, she was listed on Bureau of Naval Personnel records as single, and they could call and move her next week.

The break might be cleaner now if they accepted separation in the hope that their ordeal might end sooner. Nothing assured that. Sooner or later, one of them would have to sacrifice a career opportunity for the sake of their eventual marriage.

Rusty thought of ways to tell Allison. He knew before he hung up that he'd call Jake tomorrow and take the early transfer. He wouldn't answer, though, before consulting her. She wouldn't cry or carry on, nor would she let him delay starting the course for her. Each had chosen Navy life and its sacrifices.

She was flying this afternoon, and he had some time off. They'd agreed to meet back at the BOQ.

Allison sensed something was up as soon as she walked in.

"BUPERS called today. They want me to fill a sudden vacancy in the next class, starting in two weeks. My buddy Jake thought he was offering me a good deal."

Allison bit her lip. She put her arms around him and hugged him silently.

"I can tell Jake I can't leave now," he said. "I can ask him to give the billet to someone else and cycle me in the regular pattern in six months or so."

"No, you can't. That won't make it any easier."

"I'm sorry, Allison."

"It's not your fault. Not Jake's fault, or the Navy's fault, or anyone's fault. It's life; it's what happens. We'll survive it. I'll schedule some cross-country flights up to Pax River as soon as I can," she said. "Maybe my RAG request will move quickly, with the spotlight on women now. I might be in Norfolk earlier than we think."

"I don't know when I can fly down here," he said, "but be prepared on short notice if I find a hop or take a station aircraft for a proficiency flight.

"We only have a couple of weeks," he whispered. "Let's make the most of them."

Allison's mind raced during her early-morning run around the station. One question kept returning. Would their relationship survive this separation?

Rusty, the attractive, engaging war hero, would be a prime target for young women in Maryland. He was loyal to her, but loneliness became dangerous—it strained and tested people. Many females up there would find her man appealing.

Soaked and weary upon her return, she realized that although Rusty must go away, at least he was alive. She hadn't lost him like Michael. Hope remained, but both must work to keep love alive. Their relationship, she thought, would be stronger after it survived this.

The next two weeks sped by in a round of dinners with friends, farewell parties, and evenings alone together. Each day made their kisses more urgent.

Too bad, she thought, that people couldn't appreciate each other better in more normal times, couldn't live each day more fully when the specter of long separation wasn't upon them.

The night before he left for Patuxent River, she helped Rusty load his car. They squeezed uniforms and other miscellany of a single male officer into the trunk and backseat. Then they drove into town for a final dinner at Weidman's.

Rumors of Laramie Cox's impending washout from the flight program raged around the squadron. They ignored the storm, caught up in their own impending separation. Word of Washington intervention, angry admirals, and political heat on the commodore and the squadron CO continued to circulate. Later would be time enough to consider such things. For now, they were all that mattered.

They held hands beneath the table at Weidman's, slowly ate steak and lobster, and tried to stretch each minute together.

"I guess we either have to talk or cry," he said after a period of silence. "And crying in public is a no-no."

She laughed without humor, knowing he was right. This last night together was not one on which to hide thoughts from each other.

"This too shall pass, Rusty. The separation seems awful now, but we'll survive it, even make it work for us."

"I'm not sure how, but I'll give it my best. You know that."

"Let's pretend this is just another evening together."

"You're right—we're the ones who control that."

"Sounds okay to me," she said, her smile more radiant now.

Two hours at Weidman's went like twenty minutes. As they drove silently back through the cool, damp darkness toward the air station, Allison thought about the following day. Neither, she thought, wanted to reveal what was in their hearts. Rusty held her hand and squeezed it lightly from time to time, but said little. The ride to the base seemed to take forever.

When they pulled up before the BOQ, he took her hand as they walked slowly to her room. Allison fumbled for the key and found the keyhole in the darkness. As she stepped inside, she reached by habit for the light switch only to find Rusty's hand already over it, as the door closed behind them. The room remained dark; only the hint of music from the clock-radio on her bedside softly flavored the silence.

Back in his own room, the alarm was already set for 0500. At 6:00 A.M., Rusty would begin his drive north toward the Naval Air Test Center and Naval Air Station at Patuxent River, on Maryland's eastern shore.

Her arms moved up his back in the darkness. As she clung to the solid warmth of him, he found her lips. At first he was slow, tentative. Allison felt herself shiver lightly, although she wasn't cold. She wanted to move slowly. Tonight was a night she'd savor, dream about later, remember on lonely nights before she went to sleep. As he put his warm lips to her neck, she shuddered again and her face felt warm and flushed. She felt Rusty tremble too. They talked until each knew that they must get some rest. She insisted on getting up for his early-morning departure. When they did, both were sleepy and unrested. Each had lain awake long after the lights went out.

He kissed her again in the cool of the morning and climbed slowly into his car. "I love you, Allison," he said as though there were nothing else to say, as though they had both said it all, that each knew and no longer needed the shorthand of words. She waved until he was out of sight, then returned to her room to cry. Tomorrow evening, he would be at Patuxent River.

Chapter Twenty-six

The phone rang in Allison's room the following evening.

"I miss you," Rusty said.

"Already?"

"You mean you don't . . ."

"Of course I do." Not much to talk about after only two days, she thought, but they'd find a way.

"How was the trip?"

"Uneventful, but pretty. A nice drive, but better with the one you love."

"Everything's better with the one you love."

The chatter continued for thirty minutes. After she hung up the phone, Allison sat silently. Then she picked up the engineering book she'd selected to bore her to sleep and perused it without enthusiasm for another quarter-hour. Finally, at ten-fifteen, she decided to run until she was exhausted, to ensure that last night's sleeplessness would not recur.

Late the following afternoon, Laramie Cox paced her BOQ room, her hands clenched. *That coward,* she thought. Ted's flight aptitude report, although nicely worded and lacking either condemnation or a firm recommendation, shouted her ineptitude.

ENS Cox needs additional practice and instruction in jet aerial tactics to meet present training norms . . .

*Her landing technique requires refinement of control
and more affirmative handling of the aircraft. . . .*

Statement after weasel-worded statement chipped away
at her. When combined with those of Lieutenants O'Hara
and Douglas, and the fact that she'd already completed ten
hours of extra instruction, the report completed a picture of
failure.

She'd been twice a fool, Laramie thought. Ted had persuaded her to withdraw the charges against O'Hara. He had
checkmated her options. She could not credibly recycle the
harassment accusations against him. There must be another
way to reward Ted's perfidy.

Two weeks after Rusty O'Hara's departure, Lieutenant
Esteban Martinez reported to Training Squadron Six. A tall,
handsome Cuban-American from Miami with a black mustache, Martinez had flown F-14s for four years in fleet
squadrons. He liked good cigars, Mexican food, and independent, challenging women.

Allison was everything most previous women in his life
had not been, and she was beautiful. This one, he thought,
had brains, looks, charm, courage, and a knockout figure.
Her fire, while real, was restrained. Unencumbered by
knowledge of her involvement with Rusty, Martinez decided to court her. While not known to take no for an answer, he decided in this instance to start slowly.

The curriculum at Naval Test Pilot School, weighted toward advanced mathematics, physics, and material stress
analysis, landed heavily on Rusty, an instinctive hands-on
flier. He wished Allison, with her aeronautical engineering
background, were there to help him with the mind-bending
course work. Actually he just wished she were there.

Recently, he'd asked for help from Lieutenant Vivian
Redmond, a TPS classmate, aeronautical engineer, and Naval Academy graduate. The statuesque Philadelphia red-

head had also decided to fly fighters, and had beaten an inside track to test pilot school using every resource in her formidable inventory. Vivian, he found, always came up with the answers.

Chapter Twenty-seven

Failure had hung over Laramie's head for weeks. She shuddered when the phone call summoned her to the CO's office in the late afternoon. As she walked through the door, Commander Hardin remained seated, gesturing her to a chair in front of his desk.

"I have bad news for you, Ensign Cox," he said.

Laramie swallowed hard. Hardin swung his chair around to face her.

"I've followed your progress carefully during the past several weeks. The additional flying hours haven't improved your aerial tactics or your landings. Flight evaluation reports from your instructors show no progress. I can't send a student to carrier qualifications who can't land successfully ashore, or handle a training jet in basic aerobatics."

"What are you telling me, Commander?"

"That I have no alternative but to disenroll you from flight training."

"The stress from my encounters with O'Hara was responsible for all this," she snapped. "No woman can function when she's concerned about someone feeling . . ."

Hardin's face changed instantly and his voice lowered. "Cox, knock that off right now. You've done no better with Chadwick than you did with O'Hara. You withdrew that letter because it was a pack of lies. I had NIS investigate this matter. They've learned enough about you, and

143

some of our staff, that you'll be lucky to avoid court-martial charges of a false official statement.''

Laramie's eyes blazed; her voice shrieked. ''You and the Navy will look really great, prosecuting a failed female ensign flight student, Commander. The press will eat you for breakfast!''

''I can add insubordination, conduct unbecoming an officer, and communicating a threat to those charges if you like, Ms. Cox. Your mouth is digging a hole for you.'' Hardin's eyes riveted her. ''You'd better get out of here now, before you create more trouble for yourself.''

Halvorsen stopped Laramie on her way out of the squadron executive spaces.

''Come in and sit down for a minute,'' he said. ''I need to talk to you.''

The lanky, blond Minnesotan's conciliatory manner calmed her. Anyone sounded more friendly than the CO.

''I know the skipper had to tell you about disenrollment,'' he said, and leaned forward in his chair. ''I'm sure that hurts now, but I've seen it save people's lives. Some disenrolled officers prefer to resign their commissions if they can't fly. The bureau has been agreeable to that lately.''

''Why didn't the skipper say that?'' she snapped.

Halvorsen shrugged. ''I don't know how your conversation went with him. Anyway, that's an option.''

Laramie breathed a sigh and thought for a moment about Commander Hardin's words. Only one way out was open now.

''Have the squadron yeoman type up my resignation request,'' she said. ''I'll sign it tomorrow.''

During the interval needed to process the paperwork, they'd assign her to TRAWING ONE headquarters, Halvorsen said. Laramie drove back to the BOQ, trying to figure out how to break the news to her father. She had some unfinished business to conclude before she left Meridian.

After her disenrollment from flight training and with her

resignation request pending, Laramie began work for Cora. She made changes to classified publications and did catch-up jobs that the senior chief had put aside. Laramie's easy working days permitted enough spare time to think and plan. Life became a holding pattern.

Two weeks later, a message from the Bureau of Naval Personnel approved Laramie's resignation. She'd already turned in her flight gear and signed the documents required to disconnect herself from the service. Laramie had loaded her car for the drive to Montana, dumping uniforms into a plastic bag and jamming them behind the spare tire. Today, she wore designer slacks and a loose silk blouse. Before leaving the BOQ for the last time, she took a scrap of paper from her pocket and the telephone charge card from her purse. Laramie dialed the information operator for area code 703.

"Give me the number," she said, "for Melanie Brousseau in Leesburg, Virginia."

After the brief conversation, she pulled the door shut behind her, started her sports car, and roared out the air station gate without looking back. The sentry waved her on without saluting. The blue base registration sticker which identified her as an officer had already been scraped from the windshield of her car.

Lieutenant Esteban "Stubby" Martinez had acquired his Navy nickname from his Hispanic first name, not from his stature. He was actually tall, lean, and fit. His professional Cuban family had fled to Florida when Castro took over, years before he was born.

Word was around that Allison had a boyfriend, formerly assigned to the squadron. No harm, he decided, in testing the status of that relationship. Sometimes things changed. Coming on strong with such a woman, he knew, would be a mistake. Martinez had introduced himself and greeted Allison each day at the squadron, and joked with her on the flight line. They'd talked at the officers' club after he arrived.

"Someone told me there's a great Mexican place downtown," he said. "I'm supposed to like black beans and rice like a good Cubano, but I have this secret desire for Mexican chilis—you know, the roaring hot little ones."

"Mama Rosita's is the place," she replied. "Their chilis will turn your mouth into a flamethrower. Not fancy, but the food is great. Rusty and I went there all the time."

"Well, 'Stubby' would like to invite you to dinner there, since we both like Mexican food."

"Thanks for the invitation, but I'm still seeing Rusty. He transferred out a few weeks ago. You had no way of knowing that we have something serious going."

Long-distance romances sometimes faded, he thought, as one of his own once had.

"Nothing says we can't still be friends, Allison."

"Friends . . . sure." She smiled.

"And friends can have dinner once in a while, even if not this time?"

"Perhaps. But as you say, Stubby, another time. Thanks, anyway. You were sweet to ask."

She had taken pains, he thought, to let him down easily. He appreciated sensitivity. The setback was minor. Time remained on his side.

Someone would ask her out sooner or later, Allison thought as she drove home. Other bright young men wouldn't disappear because Rusty had transferred. Handsome, charming, quick-witted Stubby was fun to be with. If Rusty weren't her man, he'd be an attractive prospect.

Fortunately, a cross-country training flight with Ensign Broderick would let her visit Rusty in another week. Instead of the usual run into NAS Norfolk, she altered the flight plan to remain overnight at the Naval Air Test Center, Patuxent River, Maryland. Only one night, but after six weeks, even a few hours would be heavenly. Next time, she thought, she'd fly into Norfolk first to see her father.

"Stats, it's hard, but it's the only thing to do. We can't let instructors blackmail flight students or give them false hope." Giles Woodring's anger grew the more he thought about it. "It's the worst breach of integrity I've seen in a long time."

"If I know Ted Chadwick," Hardin put in, "his father would hire the sharpest Washington shyster he could find, to back up Ted's military counsel. The old man will go for our throats, even if Ted gets off. If Ted's father wasn't the tall dog on the block, we wouldn't give a second thought to reprimanding Ted." Stats Hardin also knew Admiral Chadwick's handiwork.

Hardin breathed deeply, swung around in his chair.

"As you say, Commodore, no guts, no Air Medal. Before this, I'd been hoping to make captain."

"I'll take as much of the heat for this as I can, Stats," Woodring replied. "You're not up for promotion for a couple of years. By then, old man Chadwick might be retired."

"Or promoted," Hardin said. "Guys like him lead a charmed existence. By the way, you're up for admiral yourself next year. You have plenty to lose."

"You have to live with yourself," he replied. "In the end, you do what you have to do."

Rusty sat alone near midnight in his small furnished apartment five miles from the base, his eyes bleary. He had been reading since he arrived home six hours earlier. Dinner was last night's warmed-over pizza. He'd tasted the recycled pepperoni since six o'clock.

His brain wrestled with a thick volume about aerodynamic stress factors on military airframes. The book, written by scientists, may as well have been in Martian. Endless formulae of metallurgy, airframe construction, aerodynamic design and material fatigue ran together into a slurry of mental mush. Despite several cups of coffee, his eyes began to close.

Vivian Redmond zipped through this stuff like a paperback novel, he thought. For him, each page was like chipping through granite. Only those few people in the class with aeronautical engineering backgrounds, like her, fared better. Rusty had been cautious when he asked the attractive redhead for help. She could construe that as another form of interest. The longer he was away from Allison, the greater the temptation could become.

Vivian's rounded figure and lively personality provided plenty of that. She called him "cousin," after she'd learned they both had O'Neills in their Irish family backgrounds. Were things different, he'd pursue her. But he still needed Vivian's help to survive.

Allison's impending arrival on Friday was the best news since he'd left Meridian six weeks ago. He climbed into bed and switched off the light. Three more days, he thought, seemed like forever. The demanding classwork allowed no woolgathering. Thoughts of Allison Douglas had to be on his own time.

As he stretched out, Rusty recalled his conversation with Vivian at last Friday's get-together. She'd come from a Philadelphia family who'd lived on the Main Line for generations.

"How does a woman from the Main Line end up in test pilot school?" he'd asked in the noisy bar at the Pax River Officers' Club. The tension of the week's mind-bending academics was vented nearby by loud chatter and taped rock music.

"I discovered aviation when I was twelve," Vivian said. "I was a tomboy then, seeking some great new adventure every week. My mother went critical each time I wandered off. Once I figured out that she wouldn't even know as long as I returned in time for supper, my world expanded. One day, I took the bus across town to the Philadelphia Navy Yard."

"What happened from there?" Rusty asked.

"The carrier *America* was in for a port visit. The sheer size of it blew me away. I badgered my father into taking me to the ship for public visiting that Saturday. He recognizes that as one of the great mistakes of his life. Any thought of a career in boring old investment banking disappeared once I learned about carriers, flying airplanes, Mediterranean deployments, and that people can be paid for doing what they love."

"And so one thing led to another . . ." Rusty said.

"Next thing was the Academy, then flight school, then flying CODS and S-3s out of VR-1 in Norfolk, and VR-24 out of Naples, and now here."

She graduated from the Naval Academy with Ted Chadwick's class, Rusty quickly reckoned. He'd heard she'd completed the Academy and flight school near the top of her class with a major in aeronautical engineering. During three years as a carrier-onboard-delivery, or COD, pilot with VR-1 she'd acquired a fearless reputation throughout the Atlantic Fleet.

Word was around that Big Red, as she'd become known, would bring her aircraft aboard with essential electronic parts for the ships day or night, and evacuate injured sailors to naval hospitals ashore in the worst Atlantic weather. Her career ambition, he'd heard, was to command a carrier group as a rear admiral, perhaps finish her career as Deputy Chief of Naval Operations for Air Warfare as a three-star. She was also known as someone who enjoyed life along the way.

"Let's keep the engine going on this airplane at all times while in flight, Mr. Broderick," Allison said as she and the ensign climbed into the TA-4 jet trainer for the cross-country flight north. They'd flown together several times since the crash, during which she kidded him about his talent for breaking airplanes. "Crash" Broderick hoped to change his nickname once he arrived in the fleet.

"Yes, ma'am," he said lightly, "I've tried it both ways. Keeping the engines going *does* work better."

"You'll get a look at the future today," Allison told him as they flew north. "They put new airframes and engines through their paces at Pax, test the experimental birds, and train test pilots," she said.

Broderick surely knew why she wanted to go there, she thought. Too bad they'd fly back to Meridian late tomorrow.

With few training hours in the TA-4, Broderick bounced the plane on landing at NAS Patuxent River. Certain he was already embarrassed, Allison ignored the smoky, squealing bounce. Rusty however, couldn't resist when they taxied up to the flight line.

"Hey, lady, don't you know how to drive that thing?" he shouted, smiling as the plane pulled up to the ramp.

"Sorry, Rusty, you'll have to take that up with Crash Broderick, professor of creative aviation and experimental landing technique. You should see how he flies a T-2 after a double flameout."

"I've heard, I've heard."

Broderick blushed as Rusty kissed Allison right in front of him on the tarmac.

"By the way, Lieutenant Douglas," Broderick said, "the TACAN was acting fritzy the last couple of hours. I recommend we CASREP it and get avionics here to check it out before we go back."

No one wanted to fly without a good tactical air navigation system. A casualty report would get it checked out and fixed.

"Good idea. Do that. Here's a number where you or Base Ops can reach me," she said.

She and Rusty didn't look *too* anxious to get away, she thought. When Allison picked up the parachute bag pilots used for luggage, Broderick took the hint.

"I'll get right on it," he said. After a quick salute, the ensign headed for base operations. He wouldn't mind being away from the Meridian grind for a while, she thought. With luck, he might be here long enough to get in some trouble.

Rusty looked like he wanted to kiss her again, but a busy flightline was not the place.

"You sure look good in a flight suit," he said, once they had climbed into his car. He rested his hand on her knee.

"Careful, fella. That kind of stuff got Ensign Cox in a lot of trouble, you know."

They both laughed. He reached his hand behind her head, pressed their lips together, then wrapped his arm around her. After another delightful minute, a breathless Allison whispered, "Surely there's somewhere we can go and talk."

When the door closed at his apartment, Rusty pulled her to him and kissed her again and again, wordlessly. He put his hand to her face. His warm breath in her hair made Allison feel as though she wanted to melt.

He sighed, and carried her bag to the second bedroom, which he'd decorated with two flower vases, each with a dozen red roses. While Rusty wanted her very much, one of the many things he loved about Allison was her old-fashioned determination and sense of values. That it wasn't easy for Allison either, made the situation tolerable.

Rusty's apartment telephone rang two hours later, after he'd asked her again to marry him. He handed her the phone.

"Bad news, Lieutenant," Broderick said. "The TACAN receiver is kaput and there's no spare here. NAS Norfolk can't fly a new one up here until Monday." The glee in the ensign's voice was hard to conceal.

"Yes, Mr. Broderick, that's terrible news. Are you sure you didn't jam your chewing gum into that TACAN?"

Broderick laughed.

"You caught me again, Lieutenant. Some people will do anything for a couple of extra days of liberty."

"Okay," she said, "call me when they confirm the

ETR.'' The estimated time of repair would determine when they returned to Meridian. Meanwhile, she'd send a message to VT-6 so Meridian wouldn't expect them back tomorrow. There would be copious ribbing about the breakdown. Everyone on the station knew Rusty was here.

''Bad news, huh?'' Rusty said as he slid his arms around her.

''The worst,'' she whispered as she ran her hand lightly down his face. ''No TACAN spares at Pax. We're stuck here for another two whole days. I can't imagine—'' Allison never finished the sentence. She never could talk, she thought, while Rusty was kissing her.

Chapter Twenty-eight

The weekend went too quickly, Allison thought, as she and Ensign Broderick flew above the clouds headed southwest toward Meridian on Monday afternoon. Candlelight dinners, a Sunday picnic, a driving tour of the area, and a long walk in the Maryland woods had been compressed into two days. They'd hardly seen or talked to another human being, nor spent a waking moment without holding hands.

Broderick had been silent since they took off. He must be thinking about something, or perhaps someone he'd met over the weekend. No matter, Allison thought. She had lots of her own to think about.

He broke silence about halfway to Meridian.

"Hope you had a good time up at Pax, Lieutenant."

"Sure did. How about yourself?" she said.

"I met a terrific gal, a test pilot student, last Friday night."

"A test pilot student? She must be a little older than you."

"She is, a few years, but she's great. Her name is Vivian Redmond. A redhead, smart and nice as can be. Great sense of humor, and what a looker! Being only a flight student, I can't get her to take me seriously. She turned me down for a date, even though I tried every way I know to talk her into one."

Perhaps he thought she, as his instructor and mentor, might offer some advice, Allison thought.

"Well, perhaps a quickie weekend romance wasn't for her. She knew you were leaving in a couple of days, thought she'd never see you again. Most women don't like that kind of arrangement."

"Oh, I wasn't trying for a quick weekend of passion. I'm no sweep-'em-off-their-feet lover, at least not yet. By the way, do you think we'll have another chance to come up to Pax?"

"I think so. Why not drop this Vivian a note and tell her you enjoyed meeting her, that you'd like to see her when you come up again? Perhaps she'll be flattered enough by your persistence to go out with you next time. Never hurts to try, you know."

"Hey, thanks. I didn't think of that. Nothing like getting one smart lady to help you with another," he said.

Allison returned to find a response from her assignment detailer. Half of the several hundred women pilots in the Navy must have requested transfer to carrier combat squadrons after the policy change, she thought.

A year might pass before Allison could expect transfer, and only then after a competitive screening process, the letter said. The "needs of the service" again, she thought.

Cora had phoned; so had Stubby Martinez. She decided to return Cora's call and see her later in the week. Stubby she'd keep at arm's length.

"Looks like you're about to lose at least one headache," Cora said as she and Allison sipped tea at her place two days later. "Ted Chadwick is transferring early to a desk job in Washington. I'm not supposed to know that. His rich girlfriend in Leesburg suddenly broke off with him. I'm not supposed to know *that* at all. Their relationship was a pretty hot item, maybe even marriage in the cards originally. Word may have gotten back he was fiddling around down here."

"Couldn't happen to a nicer guy," Allison replied. "He did Laramie no favors either, not that he should have."

Allison had heard enough about Ted. If she'd taken up with him, she'd have been left behind after a couple of months. The early transfer and disposable women were part of his career design, she thought.

"Ted may not have heard the last of the Laramie Cox caper. He and Cronin might be brought up on charges, you know—conduct unbecoming."

"Cronin too? How could Laramie stand him? He's dull as dirt, and smells like a burning landfill with that pipe."

"Seems that he arranged her additional flying hours," Cora said.

That explained a lot, Allison thought.

"How's Rusty doing in test pilot school?" Cora asked.

"It's tough for him. Engineering and math aren't his strong suit. He's an instinctive aviator, not a scientist."

"Maybe you're the one who should be in TPS," Cora said. "You have an aeronautical engineering degree."

"I'd like that, but first I need to get into the mainstream. I'm playing catch-up with male aviators with three years of fleet flying and a Mediterranean deployment under their belts. The next generation of women pilots won't have that problem."

"Those fleet fighter pilots will cut you zero slack out there."

"I don't *want* any slack. Some men find women aviators an affront to their macho image. That's a symptom of insecurity. There's nothing magic about flying a fighter. A challenge, yes, but not rocket science. I can handle it. I'll handle any troublemakers as well."

"Some of the trouble will come from the ones who are attracted to you," Cora said.

"Chemistry is chemistry, whether you send it to sea, or into the sky, or wherever. Human nature won't change, but neither will I become one of the boys."

Cora laughed. "You couldn't do that if you wanted to,

Allison. They won't ignore you out there. You'll have to be resigned to that."

Allison shrugged. "I wish I could get them to ignore me here," she said.

"Someone trying to move in on Rusty's territory?"

"No, this one's honest enough. We acquired a new pilot named Stubby Martinez a couple of weeks after Rusty transferred. Good-looking, nice man. You could even call him a hunk. He doesn't want to understand that Rusty and I still love each other. After one firm but polite waveoff, he's still orbiting."

"That will happen anywhere, until you and Rusty are stationed together again, or married. The other danger is women who want to snare Rusty. He's mighty attractive."

"I trust him."

"He's also human, Allison. Being this far away makes him vulnerable."

"You're talking gland-type vulnerable, lonely-type vulnerable. Okay, I understand that. Men aren't the only ones who get that way."

Cora smiled.

Ensign Broderick walked into the base exchange flower shop at Meridian on Tuesday afternoon.

"I'd like to send two dozen red roses to this lady," he said, handing Vivian's name and home address to the clerk.

"She must be a very special lady to rate *two* dozen roses, at these prices," the woman replied.

"Yes, she is that. I hope she'll think about them as you did."

The woman smiled, wrote out the wire, and took his credit card.

"I almost forgot," she said. "How do you want the card signed? You want her to know who they're from."

"Just sign it 'an admirer.' She'll know who it is." That would be sophisticated and cool, Broderick thought.

* * *

Allison had been gone only a week and already he missed her as though she hadn't been there at all, Rusty thought. At eleven P.M. he studied hard as ever as the technical material became tougher. Without Allison nearby, he was pleased not to have much spare time. This consuming curriculum kept him out of trouble. Tomorrow, he'd break with the grind and have a proper dinner at the officers' club.

After a day of flying with an instructor, wringing out an F-18 to simulate test conditions, Rusty was ready for a double-sized prime rib. Wednesday prime rib nights drew customers. Soon after he walked into the bar, he saw Vivian. Her back was to him, but the luxuriant red hair was unmistakable.

A few minutes later, she came to the bar.

"Hello, cousin," she said, eyes sparkling. The standard greeting had even more than the usual enthusiasm.

"Hi, Vivian. What's going on?" he replied, not expecting much of an answer.

"How are you enjoying nondestructive material stress analysis?" she said. His pained expression must have shown.

"More fun than drowning puppies," he replied. "Another book written in Swahili."

"I had trouble with it too," she said, "until I figured out a couple of the formulas. Once you do that, there's a shortcut to the others."

"I'd sure like to know how you did that. If I don't get smart about it quick, I'm in deep kimchi." From his classroom answers the past few days, Vivian might have figured that out, he thought.

"I'll be happy to share it with you. It takes about an hour."

Rusty saw a way out of his academic dilemma.

"Tell me when you have an hour to spare and I'll be all ears."

"Tonight," she said.

"Great," he replied. "Let's fortify ourselves with a couple of these prime ribs first. Have to prepare for the mental exertion.''

''It's a deal, cousin,'' she said.

Vivian's apartment was ten minutes from Rusty's, an upscale two-bedroom with antiques, fine furniture, and a large, comfortable sofa. A Waterford crystal vase held a gigantic spray of roses garnished with baby's breath. The lady from the Main Line wasn't living on a Navy lieutenant's salary, he thought.

''What beautiful roses,'' he said.

''Thank you,'' she replied, smiling somewhat strangely at him.

When he sat next to her, Rusty smelled her subtle, slightly musky perfume. He saw the smooth skin of her face as the soft lilt of her voice explained with logical simplicity the mind-bending material stress formulas.

Not the gregarious Vivian of daylight hours out in the world. Not the businesslike Vivian of test pilot hops and proficiency flying. In this more intimate atmosphere, he had difficulty keeping his mind on the formulas. She was, he thought, as brilliant as she was beautiful.

''So, it's really not hard once we get past the chaff the theorists throw up to distract us,'' she said.

''Easy for you engineers,'' Rusty replied, ''but I'm only a carefree old fighter pilot. I never even built a model airplane when I was a kid. Analyzing airframes into a coma is difficult for me.''

She laughed. ''If you want to know, I didn't build models either. No one told me I had to.''

Rusty looked at his watch. Already 2230, he thought. Lingering here would only get him in trouble.

Chapter Twenty-nine

Allison's early-morning run through the base a few days after her return from Pax River included a surprise.

"Good morning," a deep voice said behind her. When she turned, Stubby Martinez, in jogging shorts and a T-shirt, ran along close behind. He came out of one of the side streets, she thought. The brief outfit confirmed his fit, muscular physique. Beads of light perspiration made his face glow.

"Mind if I run with you?" he said.

"Sure, come on." These daily runs became a lonely ordeal when Rusty left.

Her baggy, gray sweatsuit, unlike Stubby's brief outfit, revealed little of her figure. And the perspiration that matted her hair did little to enhance her attractiveness.

"Do you jog every day?"

"Most days," she replied, "whenever I find time. It's a good unwinder after flying."

"Yes," he said, "some students are more stress-inducing than others. Could we ever have been that bad during flight training?" he quipped.

When she arrived back at the BOQ, Allison decided to vary her route and time. Nonetheless, she encountered Martinez three mornings during the next two weeks. Ever pleasant, he didn't press his luck. Good thing, she thought. Her life was already complex enough.

* * *

Stats Hardin was certain that Ted Chadwick had spoken to his father. Chadwick seemed confident, even cocky, as he strode into the CO's office.

Hardin looked up from his seat behind the desk, leaving Chadwick standing.

"Ted, I resent when one of my officers forces me to discipline him."

"Then why do so, Commander? I probably shouldn't have dated Laramie, but that didn't affect my judgment in writing her flight aptitude report. Nothing anyone could have done would get that woman through flight training. Believe me, I tried. It's not worth falling on our swords about." Chadwick's words implied Stats Hardin would pay if anything happened to Ted's career.

Hardin's eyes narrowed.

"Mr. Chadwick, you've just compounded a serious error in judgment with an appalling lack of integrity, a gross underestimation of what you did, marginal insubordination, and insufferable arrogance. You've messed up big-time. I have enough evidence of your cozy little arrangement with Laramie to convict you ten times over of conduct unbecoming an officer. You should have stuck to chasing the town girls, Ted."

Ted's expression suddenly changed.

"Sir, I—"

"Chadwick, in case you forgot, your only answer is 'I have no excuse, sir.' I haven't heard that from you yet."

"Sir, I will never do this again." Chadwick's voice tremored now.

Hardin hesitated a moment, breathing deeply as though thinking hard. Then he fixed the lieutenant with a withering stare and said, "You're right about that. You won't."

"Say, Lieutenant Douglas, if you're doing another cross-country to Pax River, I'd like to go along." Ensign Broderick found Allison in the squadron office.

"How about late next week? This time, we'll stop at

NAS Norfolk. But don't break the TACAN again, or anything else . . . at least until we get to Pax.''

"Roger that, Ms. Douglas. I'll set her down really easy in Norfolk.''

"You'd better. The pilot who'll meet us on the ramp has more flight hours and landings than this whole squadron put together. My father spent more time in a pay line than this whole crowd has in a chow line.''

Rusty saw the test pilot course as a relentless blizzard of technical information. He'd turned several times to Vivian for help. Other classmates also answered questions for him, but none had her incisive quickness, her uncanny ability to decipher complex engineering theory. His stupidity, fortunately, would keep her from being attracted to him, he thought.

Vivian's femininity, though, was difficult to ignore. The subtle, delightful smell of her when she moved close to illustrate a point when they shared a textbook distracted him. She was another brilliant, beautiful woman aviator. But he didn't want another one. He already loved the one he had.

To keep himself honest, Rusty decided to short himself out with Vivian by describing his relationship with Allison. That might end her helpfulness, but he must take that chance.

He didn't trust himself after being alone for the past two weeks. Fortunately, Allison would fly up Friday.

"My fiancée is coming up this weekend from Meridian on a cross-country,'' he said as he and Vivian took a break from studying wind tunnel theory.

"I didn't realize you were engaged, Rusty,'' she said. Her face showed surprise.

"You'll meet her Friday afternoon. She's great—really something. Very much like you in many ways.'' He wasn't sure that had come out as he intended.

The disappointment in Vivian's face was subtle. Maybe

she would avoid the Friday gathering at the club, or perhaps go to see who he found so attractive. On second thought, Vivian would not shrink from challenge.

When Allison landed at NAS Norfolk, her father stood on the ramp, hands cupped over his ears as the TA-4 taxied up with a whistling roar. A stone's throw away, she thought, she'd first watched F-4s taking off, and decided she wanted to be a fighter pilot. After she hugged Doug, she sent Ensign Broderick to do the paperwork at base operations.

Allison had not seen her father in six months, although she often wrote and called. She wanted to tell him in person about Rusty.

"Redheaded Irish fighter pilot with a DFC, and at test pilot school no less," he said, seeming only a little surprised. She suspected he knew this day would come.

"You'll like him, Dad."

She'd told him he would like Michael Nelson too, she thought.

"Allison, you've always had good sense. I'm sure Rusty O'Hara is a fine fellow. When can we get him down here for dinner?"

"Next trip for sure. We're kind of pinched this time." She bit her lip, knowing that she selfishly wanted Rusty to herself this weekend.

Doug surely wanted to know about her intentions and timing, she thought, but she didn't know herself. She only knew that she loved Rusty O'Hara, and, Doug or not, she craved to get in the airplane and fly to Pax River.

They chatted while Broderick preflighted the aircraft.

"Allison, you sure called it right on women in combat squadrons. I thought that policy change was years away."

She shrugged. "My confidence was only a guess, mixed with wishful thinking. With the full RAG training pipeline, I'm not nearly there yet, only closer. Rusty and I haven't figured how we'll work this out either."

"Take your time. You won't be rushed into anything, if I know you."

Doug gave advice artfully, without seeming to, she thought.

After a half-hour, with hugs and good-byes to her father, she had Broderick taxi the aircraft onto the white concrete runway. Twenty minutes later, they landed at Pax River. Her student made an extra effort, she thought, not to bounce the airplane this time.

Rusty dashed over during his lunch break to welcome her. Classes held him captive for another two hours. As Broderick hastily departed, Rusty kissed and hugged her, his hands warm on her back as he pulled her to him, lips warm against hers. She no longer cared if he embraced her on the ramp in front of everyone. Life was too short, their time together too precious. Minutes later, he pressed the car and apartment keys into her hand, then raced off reluctantly to his next class.

Allison showered and stretched out for a nap. The hectic week and the early launch to fly up this morning had tired her. She didn't hear Rusty come in. When his lips touched her neck, she opened her eyes only for a moment, sighed, then stretched her arms out to enfold him. The pang of longing coursed through her as she pulled him close, felt his strong arms close quickly around her. Neither said a word.

When they arrived at the officers' club, the noisy bar was full of aviators celebrating the end of a hard week and the upcoming weekend. Wives and some girlfriends were salted among the males. Modern jazz painted a chaotic overlay of sound over the buzz of conversation. Hors d'oeuvres and popcorn were almost gone.

Rusty introduced Allison to his classmates. That would assure everyone, including Vivian, that she was real, and confirm to all that he was indeed "taken."

The test pilot trainees, Allison noticed, were a mixed bag. Some, like Rusty, were open and gregarious. Others were serious, almost shy. A few seemed brooding and aloof. Most were married. Allison gathered from the conversations that no one had an easy time academically.

Of the three women in the class, Vivian Redmond was the only one who drew her attention. Vivian was an inch taller and fifteen pounds heavier than she, but fit, her curves more pronounced. The woman's quick intellect and interest in her made Allison feel scrutinized by the competition. They spoke as Rusty fetched fresh drinks. No wonder Broderick was so taken with her, Allison thought.

"What's on your dream sheet, Allison?" she asked.

"The RAG and a fleet seat out of Norfolk should put Rusty and me close enough to tie the knot," she said. She wanted to leave no doubt.

"Replacement Air Group seats are tough to find now. The new policy on women will make that even harder."

Vivian would compete for a fleet job after she graduated from test pilot school, Allison thought. The school provided a great advantage.

"True, but I have plenty of jet time and good tickets. If I can't snag one, I'll try to come here, then try again."

"An aeronautical engineering degree helps a lot at TPS," Vivian said. "Rusty has said more than once that he wishes he had more technical background."

"I believe it," she replied. Vivian could learn another way that she already had the engineering degree.

Rusty's need for help made Allison yearn to be there. By the time she got to Pax, she thought, he'd either have finished the course or perhaps be past her ability to help him.

"The school sounds exciting, but I'd rather have a fighter squadron tour first," Allison said.

"The way the world goes these days, you might get combat time out in the fleet," Vivian said. She shrugged.

"No point flying fighters unless you're ready for combat,'' she replied. ''I don't start fights, but I can finish them.''

Rusty returned, balancing three fresh drinks. Vivian soon excused herself. Ensign Broderick, Allison noticed, had been waiting in the corner for his opportunity to approach her.

''What that woman doesn't know about engineering theory isn't worth knowing,'' Rusty said as he watched Vivian walk away.

''She seems very bright, in addition to being good-looking,'' Allison said.

''Vivian's helped me a lot on the theoretical stuff, the formulas, stress analysis, wind tunnel equations. You know, the mind-benders.''

Allison knew the material. The science had been difficult for her in college, harder than it appeared to be for Vivian Redmond. There was no way to ask where they studied without appearing jealous. The Redmond woman was not one a normal man could ignore. The thought of them studying together sat uneasily with her, but he needed help, and she couldn't be here to provide it.

As they drove home after dinner, Allison asked him how TPS was going.

''More unfamiliar material every day,'' he said with a sigh. ''If I'd studied engineering in college, that would help. It's a grind, but the flying is good.

''What's new at Meridian? Aside from Laramie Cox being gone.''

''Nothing much. Ted will be short-toured, and I hear from Cora that he and Cronin might get captain's mast over the business with Laramie. I'm not sure if the transfer's because of the trouble, or whether he and 'Admiral Daddy' planned it all along. We also picked up another instructor after you left.''

''Who's that?''

''Stubby Martinez, a fighter pilot lieutenant from the fleet.''

"I don't know him. What's he look like?"

"Tall, dark, slender, black mustache, Cuban-American."

"Charming, debonair, devastatingly handsome?"

"He's a nice man, good-looking."

"What you girls call a hunk?"

"About like any normal girl would call *you* a hunk." Allison reached across the car seat and began rubbing the back of his neck. She knew he liked that. His neck muscles were tense. His sudden interest in Martinez, and the lack of reaction to the fate of his former rival, interested her. Perhaps it paralleled her interest in Vivian.

"What kind of pilot is Vivian?" Allison asked.

"She's been a reciprocating engine COD pilot up to now, has some S-3 jet time. Capable, but not aggressive tactically," he mumbled. "But she wasn't trained as a fighter pilot either."

"Only Attila the Hun could be more aggressive in a fighter than you are, Rusty," she said. "Perhaps you're too critical."

"Her strong suit is engineering," he said. "Everyone has strengths. I fly more aggressively; she knows science better."

Allison wondered about Vivian's other talents. She also suspected that Vivian would go after Rusty. The tutoring gave her a definite advantage, even a hold on him. Allison hadn't been joking when she told Rusty most normal women would find him a hunk.

Chapter Thirty

As the TA-4 with Allison and Ensign Broderick taxied out into the twilight from the NAS Patuxent River flight line, Rusty stood and watched. He waited in the growing darkness until the roar of the engines faded and the glint of the plane's warning lights told him they had lifted off and headed south, then turned back toward his car. The weekend had been too short.

Rusty pulled from his pocket the rumpled letter from a TRARON SIX buddy. The news didn't mention Ted Chadwick's shortened tour, but reported that Stubby Martinez and Allison had jogged several times on the base together. She hadn't mentioned that, which bothered him. He tried to convince himself that Allison wouldn't stray. Rusty remembered the patience it took to woo her. Perhaps she too was affected by the irrationality that sometimes accompanied loneliness.

Allison had been especially affectionate this weekend, he thought, more so than last time, when they'd been separated longer. Why would she come up here if another interest bloomed at Meridian? She was honest enough to call things off if her affections changed.

Rusty recalled his meetings with Vivian, how much they'd been engineering tutorials, and how much of them he'd enjoyed because she was a beautiful, vital woman. Despite that, he had done nothing. He'd passed up recent options to go flying with her, although they'd been together on three scheduled training flights. Often lately, he'd wished Vivian was a homely, snaggletoothed hag.

Allison and Vivian had enough time to take the measure of each other Friday night. Aside from acknowledging Vivian's obvious attractiveness, Allison had said nothing about her.

He sat and thought for several minutes in the cool darkness. Then he turned the key and drove slowly toward home.

By Thursday night, Rusty knew he must ask Vivian's help again. He was in deep academic weeds, and aware that he was sailing into shoal water by asking her. His survival instinct had wrestled caution to the ground. The following day at the Friday afternoon get-together they discussed equations dealing with airframe stress.

"Allison's not coming up this weekend?" Vivian asked. Her question sounded matter-of-fact. He knew it wasn't.

"No. If she were, we'd spend the weekend doing my homework."

"Allison's an engineer, then?"

"She worked six years for an AE degree in Norfolk before she came in. Went to college nights and weekends, worked days."

"She didn't mention that. More power to her. Okay, I'm ginning up five-alarm chili tomorrow. Come over about six and bring some soda. We'll get those equations under control."

Vivian's response sounded friendly enough, although he wasn't sure she'd honor Allison's territorial claim. He had to keep himself in check and ensure he didn't inadvertently set off sparks between them.

At three minutes past six the following evening, he appeared with text and notebook in one hand and a cold liter of soda in the other. The aroma of spices and jalapeños wafted out from the kitchen. Soft mariachi music drifted from quad-stereo speakers. Black slacks and an embroidered red silk blouse showed Vivian off to advantage. Long, shining red hair, usually in a tight bun to conform to uniform regulations, cascaded over her shoulders.

"Come on in, the fire is only starting," she said, holding up a hot red pepper. Rusty silently noted that that was an understatement.

"I really appreciate your help, Vivian. You have better things to do with Saturday nights than tutor spacey liberal arts majors in aeronautical engineering."

She smiled.

That had not come out right, he thought. "Where can I put the soda?"

"Slip it in the fridge; we'll have it with dinner. The Margaritas Viviana on the top shelf are my own recipe."

He hoped he hadn't made a bad mistake.

Vivian deftly handled the large skillet containing ingredients for *biftec en salsa roja* and added chopped peppers and salt.

"Here, taste this," she said, bringing him a wooden spoonful of the piquant sauce. Her warm fragrance next to him overruled his taste buds. The sauce could have been anything for all he knew. Hot chilies made his mouth tingle.

"It's great," he said. "Where did you learn to cook Mexican like this?"

"I lived at Lake Chapala near Guadalajara one summer before I came in the Navy. The food is wonderful there." Her eyes sparkled as they met his.

"Go ahead and pour the margaritas," she said. "This will have to cook down for a while."

Her veranda overlooking the Maryland woods held a table for two set with silver, linen, and crystal. A candle provided the only light.

"Pretty elaborate lashup for five-alarm chili," Rusty remarked good-naturedly.

"Life's too short not to enjoy every good thing," she said, sliding into the opposite seat, margarita in hand. "I changed the menu."

"To the chef," he said, raising the glass.

"And the evening," she murmured.

Her margaritas were powerful but subtle. The mariachi music made the place seem exotic. Getting back to equations might be difficult. On the other hand, he'd been clear about Allison and his commitment to her.

The growing darkness, lit only by the candle, enhanced Vivian's attractiveness. The shining red hair framed her face and accented her warm smile. Her perfume, carried on the night air, was subtle, provocative.

The spicy food steamed with exotic aromas. A light breeze whipped the candle. He remembered that spicy dishes were considered an aphrodisiac in some countries. Not that he needed any, he thought.

"Seems a long way from equations," he said.

"Yes," she said. "The important ones aren't in the engineering books, anyway."

She had changed course, he thought.

"Sometimes urgency drives the problem instead of importance," Rusty said, trying to lower the level of abstraction. "Life's a one-step-at-a-time drill."

"Yes, and a one-tile-at-a-time mosaic. I want a large mosaic to look back upon one day, a rich one with every space filled in with something colorful."

Vivian was as skilled with imagery as equations. He must keep his hands on the tiller of the conversation, and off her, he thought.

After dinner, Rusty was ill-prepared for study. As the mariachi music continued softly, they sat on her large sofa to work the engineering lesson. She set the book on the large glass-topped coffee table and spread notes out nearby.

Vivian explained each formula in turn. He felt like a blind man for not capturing the concepts earlier. She made it seem so easy.

"How did I ever get an airplane off the ground without all this?" he mumbled.

"Some people who understand this, and more, could

never fly an airplane,'' she said, engaging his eyes. Her own sparkled now in the half-darkness. ''Of those who are pilots, few could handle a fighter. Of them, only a handful would survive combat.''

She sought to boost his morale, he thought. He understood how Laramie felt when mastery of jet aircraft evaded her.

''Equations will never be my bag,'' he said, ''but there's no other way.''

She put her warm, smooth hand lightly on his.

''This too shall pass, Rusty,'' she said softly.

His face felt hot. Perhaps it was red. He remembered when Allison had said the same thing not long ago, with a very different meaning.

After a few seconds, Vivian removed her hand. They continued the discussion about equations. By the time she had deciphered the formulas for him and he'd scrawled the explanations into his notebook, it was eleven-thirty. She had saved him again, he thought.

She hadn't made any overt moves toward him, but Rusty felt she was capable of it. But Vivian had her pick of the single men in the class. Why him, who'd declared himself about Allison? Rusty thought.

''You don't need beauty sleep, but I do,'' he said, making light of his attempt to escape.

She walked with him to the door.

''I don't know how to thank you, again, for the help . . . and for the wonderful dinner.'' He took her hand, hoping his agitation didn't show in his voice. ''You have my grateful IOU for the best steakhouse or seafood place on the Eastern Shore. I really owe you one . . . more than one.''

''My pleasure,'' she said, showing no outward sign that she wanted their relationship to be anything else.

Rusty turned to leave, gently releasing her hand.

''Rusty?''

He turned back to look at her. Her eyes gleamed a little more now.

"Allison Douglas is a very lucky woman," she said.

"Good night," he whispered, and was gone.

When he opened the door, the answering machine blinked its red light at him in the darkness. Two messages from Allison, one a scant half-hour before. He wondered if she was still up. Instinct pressed him to call anyway.

"I hope I didn't get you up," he said when a sleepy Allison answered.

"What time is it?"

"About midnight."

"I thought you'd be home tonight," she said.

"I'm in trouble with airframe stress formulas and equations again. I don't get this stuff. We're being tested on it Monday."

There was no response. He continued.

"Vivian agreed to help me out again. I was over at her place tonight being tutored."

"Is that what you call it?" she said.

"Hey, wait a minute! If you're insinuating I was over there for anything else, you're dead wrong." Rusty's anger rose. Time to get a grip on himself. He was especially spun up after evading Vivian's subtle but real offer.

"Am I supposed to believe that the only one who can help you is the most attractive woman in the class? No one else knows airframe stress analysis in that whole brain trust of test pilots? Have you *tried* any of the men?" Allison sounded fully awake now, and angry.

"I've tried to get help from several of the men. None understand the concepts nearly as well. If I'd gone over there for any other reason, I wouldn't be here. I also wouldn't have told you the truth about where I've been. Even a dumb fighter pilot can think up a cover story. What is this, Allison?"

"The way Vivian looked at you when I was up there last week told me she wants you, Rusty. That doesn't take equations."

Allison was right, but the implication infuriated him. She didn't know what he'd been through with Vivian tonight. Sure she'd wanted him tonight, but he couldn't tell Allison that.

"So now you think that she has what she wanted, is that it? Tell me about your jogging buddy Stubby Martinez, Allison. Am I supposed to be pleased about him?"

The phone was silent for a moment.

"I've run into Stubby several times in the morning. You know I jog every day. So does he. I don't go out with him, or look for him. He finds me out there by coincidence." Allison had not asked how he found out, or denied that she had done so. Her words sounded awkward, defensive.

"Well, I don't like your implications about me and Vivian. That's great trust and confidence, Allison, just terrific. And I have to learn from someone else about your jogs with Martinez. If you're being so all-fired upfront, why didn't you tell me that last week when you were up here?"

"There's nothing to tell. It isn't important; that's why I didn't mention it!" Her voice sounded shrill.

"Important enough for someone to write to me about."

"Whoever wrote to you has a dirty mind."

"Nonsense, Allison, he's just reporting facts. You were jogging with Martinez."

"You're jealous, you're really jealous."

"And you're not? Hey, I told you where I was tonight, and you accuse me of fooling around. I'd have to be pretty stupid or terminally nervy to carry that off. You're doing neither of us any favors with talk like that, Allison. You're the one with the dirty mind."

Rusty's fury grew. He hadn't started this. Had he taken Vivian up on her tacit offer, this conversation wouldn't be happening. Rusty had refused her out of the most noble motives. The abuse he was taking for it now fueled his anger. More talk might only make it worse.

"Allison," he said, "when you get your act together,

you call me. We don't have anything else to talk about now. Good night.''

Rusty put the phone down gently, not that he wanted to. Allison would come to her senses. He knew she wasn't fooling around with Martinez. She needed to understand it wasn't easy for him either. If this problem resolved, he'd spend some time one afternoon telling this smart woman aviator from Norfolk about men.

Chapter Thirty-one

Slowly, Allison hung up the phone. Perhaps she was wrong. Vivian certainly wanted Rusty. No woman could deceive another about that. Women would continue to be attracted to him.

He'd been furious at her. Her sudden reaction may have torn him loose. The next move was hers, he said.

Broderick's comments cycled through her mind. The unhappy ensign had again tried to court Vivian. She'd made clear her romantic interest was a member of her test pilot class. Allison knew which one.

As she lay awake at one in the morning, Allison reviewed Rusty's phone call. She'd blown it. If Rusty wasn't guilty, he *should* be furious. His comments about her and Martinez, much more benign, had roused her indignation immediately. She didn't intend to alienate him—she didn't know exactly *what* she had meant.

Perhaps she should call Rusty back and apologize. No. He'd been quick to accuse her. He shouldn't have done that. Whoever wrote to Rusty about Stubby was small-minded, but the old boy network protected their own. Let him stew for a while, she thought. She couldn't forget the conversation. Sleep evaded her.

Before dawn, Allison arose and made coffee. Ugly dreams had punctuated restless napping.

When she ran at sunrise, she saw only a lone security vehicle. She wondered what Rusty might do if he were angry enough. If he went to Vivian, the redhead would win him by default. Rusty's continued need for engineering help would cinch that. With her other attributes, Vivian didn't need academics to hold him.

If Rusty broke their relationship off, Allison knew she would have no problem finding a man. She didn't want that. Right now, she wanted Rusty's arms around her, wanted their relationship to be right again.

He, however, mustn't take her for granted. He could not find her apology a sign of weakness, or of willingness to defer to him in the future. She controlled her life; she wouldn't be spoken to like that.

When she returned exhausted, miles later, to the BOQ, she stretched out, hoping for dreamless sleep. Finally, she nodded off. At ten-thirty the jangling phone awakened her.

Rusty had called to apologize, she thought. She waited until the fourth ring, not wanting to seem anxious. Allison hadn't even considered what she'd say. She'd hold out, then forgive him.

"Allison?" the voice said.

"Yes."

"Stubby Martinez. I was going to brunch at the officers' club in a while. Would you like to come along?"

Allison had to think fast. She sat up in bed.

"Good idea, Stubby. I'd planned to go myself. I'll meet you down front at the BOQ in a half-hour if that's okay."

Whoever had snitched to Rusty about their jogs in the mornings would go critical over brunch at the officers' club.

They talked and ate for two hours. He led bright conversation from current events to geopolitics, and told her about his family in Miami. His warm mixture of Latin and North American culture made her feel valued. If Stubby were making a run, she thought, he was doing so with charm and class.

Afterward, they drove into the countryside. She showed him local places she'd visited with Rusty. More than once, she wondered what Rusty was doing, whether he had called. Martinez returned her to the BOQ in the late afternoon, took her hand in both of his, and pressed it lightly when they parted. A nice way to spend the day when her world had turned inside out.

Allison opened the door and stepped into her dimly lit room. She saw only the steady red light on the answering machine. No one had called. She'd phone Rusty, but then decided to wait. Finally, she knew she'd made a terrible mistake last night.

For years Rusty O'Hara had curbed his temper. Such volatility, if uncontrolled, could destroy him. Gulf War combat taught him to regard his enemy with the unemotional detachment of an arcade game, to rigidly suppress emotion's fatal irrationality. He owed his life to his success in doing that.

He'd sat for a moment after hanging up the phone and stared at the instrument.

"Allison," he shouted, glad that the building had concrete walls, "why couldn't you trust me? If I were going to play around with Vivian, I'd just do it. You'd know nothing about it!"

He picked up the heavy book on airframes and threw it against the wall. What a fool he'd been to call Allison.

Nothing in his life had humiliated him as much as Allison's accusation. He'd resisted one of the most attractive temptations ever for her. Things would be different now if he hadn't kept his word. There'd been no reward for that.

As his anger subsided, he considered calling Vivian. If he went to her, he couldn't turn back. His next conversation with Allison would tell her they had nothing more to talk about.

He recalled last weekend's tender moments. How could life change so radically in a week? Accused of being unfaithful, he wondered if he should observe the Irish proverb that said one may as well be hanged for a sheep as a lamb.

He soon realized the idea came from his hurt at Allison's

ill-chosen words. No one would force him to act rashly, even himself. He'd decide later. If nothing changed by morning, he might call Vivian and invite her to brunch.

The morning was no better. What a fool he'd have been to give up test pilot school for Allison. Something like this would only have happened later. He made some double-strength coffee.

At seven forty-five, he wondered if Allison was up yet. Then he wondered if Vivian were still in bed now. He knew it was time to think about something else.

After three cups of coffee, Rusty took a cold shower, pulled on old clothes, and walked to his car. He drove north over country roads toward the Bay Bridge, then turned down a scenic road to St. Michael's, Maryland.

After lunch, he walked for hours along the Chesapeake Bay, scanning the water, the boats, and the shore. When he returned to the car, he'd decided not to call Allison.

Chapter Thirty-two

The sun dipped into the west late Sunday afternoon as Allison looked at her watch. It was 4:30 P.M. Rusty hadn't called. He might already be over at Vivian's. That may have been where he'd intended to be, after her rash words last night. She bit her tongue.

The hours since they spoke seemed like a week. Allison knew she should have kept her mouth shut. Jealousy caused this. Only she was to blame.

She should have called Rusty last night and apologized. Eating crow came bitterly hard, especially with the most important person in your life.

One choice remained. Either call him or not. After this, she could blame no one else. Allison put her face in her hands for a long moment. Then she picked up the telephone.

She could tell from the first ring that Rusty wouldn't answer. Strange how a telephone sometimes tells you that, she thought. No answering machine came on. Either he hadn't unpacked it yet, or the device was off.

Five o'clock. Maybe he was at Vivian's, she thought with a pang. Or perhaps they were at his place, with the phone disconnected. Now that she was prepared to humiliate herself, Allison thought, the telephone wouldn't let her.

She called again at five-thirty. No answer.

Her stomach ached as she hung up the phone. Allison paced across the room for a few minutes, then went out and walked near the BOQ for fresh air.

179

At six Rusty's line was busy. She wondered who he was talking to, when he'd come in, whether he'd been there all the time.

She called ten minutes later. This time the phone rang.

"O'Hara," the voice said.

"It's me, Rusty." She heard a deep breath on the other end.

"Your quarter," he said.

"I said a lot of dumb, unfair things last night, and I'm sorry."

"Is that all?"

"I don't know what to say except that I was wrong. I didn't intend to hurt you. I was jealous and catty and mean, and I apologize."

"Is that all?"

"I love you, Rusty." She heard another deep breath.

"Now we're getting somewhere."

The O'Hara charm and optimism were still missing from his voice.

"And I don't think you were doing anything with Vivian Redmond except studying engineering."

"You're sure about that."

"Absolutely. I'm sorry I implied anything else, and I apologize." Allison bit her tongue again. The crow tasted awful but this was the only way.

Rusty didn't answer immediately.

"We must stop this or it will destroy us," he said.

"I know."

"We must be together again, somehow, somewhere. You can't be jealous about me with people like Vivian, and I can't worry about poachers like Martinez."

"I know," she said. Rusty was right. She almost defended Martinez, but this wasn't the time.

"I didn't mean to nick you about him. I was hurt. I'm sorry."

"It's all right, Rusty."

". . . and I've got to find a new tutor around here."

"I said I trust you, Rusty."

"I'm not sure that I trust me, or Vivian. She's human too, and she's quite a woman in addition to being a superb engineer. Vivian's a good person. She has normal emotions like everyone else. No one can blame her for that."

". . . and she's attracted to you."

"Yes, I think she is."

"I could see it in her eyes the last time I was up there."

"You women see these subtle things we men don't even look for. We can be a little dense, you know."

Allison began to relax.

"Let's think about what we do now," he said.

Neither of them had figured it out past this point, she thought.

"We'll talk in another day or two."

"I love you, Rusty."

"I love you too. Was there ever any doubt of that?"

"For a little while I wasn't sure, but I was wrong. Anyone can be wrong once in a while."

"You picked the wrong thing to be wrong about. Try anything else in the world next time you decide to screw up. Anything."

"I wish I could be there with you right now," she said.

"Me too."

Early the next morning, she drove to the squadron office and dialed the AUTOVON phone number for the aviation detailing branch of the Bureau of Naval Personnel.

She'd sat up for four hours after her call with Rusty, alternately relieved and unsure. Finally, only one decision remained if she'd have the life she wanted now. Not the life she started out to want. Her objectives, she realized, had grown.

Her original career plan hadn't included Michael and Rusty. Maybe it should have, but she was younger and more stubborn then. Perhaps she wouldn't have come this far had she not been that way.

"The Air Station side of Pax River, Allison?" the assignment detailer said. "Everyone wants the test pilot school." She heard the riffling of papers in the background.

"I'll take TPS if you've got it," she said.

"Sure. Send in a fifty-pound box of 'attaboys' and a certificate that you walk on water in sea state seven, and I'll send you a discount coupon for a set of orders," the detailer replied. Sea state seven was a full-blown hurricane at sea.

Allison suspected the detailer was flipping through printouts and computer screens to find assignments coming open at Pax River.

"Are you S-3 qualified?" he asked offhandedly, obviously examining the aviation requirements for some job. Some versions of the jet antisubmarine warfare plane had been modified to take the place of the carrier onboard delivery COD, to make it an administrative aircraft.

"Not yet, but I have enough jet hours and carrier traps to learn the S-3 in record time. Lots of T-39, A-4, T-2, and C-2 time. Learning S-3s should be a breeze." She wanted to give the detailer every reason to make the assignment work.

She heard an electronic bleep in the background as the assignment officer sorted through the personnel database.

"Might have something. You know a gal named Eleanor Hart?"

"Sure, Ellie got married about a year ago. Where is she now?"

"She flies the station S-3 at Pax River. She's requested to be taken off flight status now that she's growing a basketball. That might be your chance."

Allison was happy for more than one reason that her friend was anticipating motherhood.

"I'm looking at your duty preference card. A few weeks ago, you asked for the RAG and a fleet fighter squadron. That's a long way from station aircraft at Pax River."

"Would 'personal reasons' be okay?" she said.

"Sure, but this might make the RAG tougher to get later. You could fall into a fleet seat from there, or be out of the pattern. No telling now. It's a gamble."

"Life's a gamble. What can I tell you?"

"When can you roll out of Meridian?"

"Tomorrow morning."

"You're taking a chance. Station S-3 drivers don't draw much water for fleet seats or school assignments. Your instructor job looks better for that from here."

"I'll take Pax River. Can you fix it?"

"I'll put it in with the placement people. We'll know in a few days. I'll give you a growl when it comes back. A relief for you will be easy. Plenty of fleet pilots are rotating ashore now."

"Great, I'll wait for your call."

"He must be some guy, Allison."

"How did you know?"

"It's always a guy or a gal when people like you do things like this. I had a hotshot fighter jock call up a few weeks ago who wanted to extend at Meridian after landing orders to TPS."

"Yes, I know him. He *is* quite a guy."

"That's funny. He said he wanted to stay there because of a terrific girl."

"Well, at least one of them was right," she said.

"This means another aircraft qualification to broaden your record. You could pick up a couple more at Pax. You're also recommended for test pilot school. Pretty good for a Lt (jg). You may have a better shot at a fleet seat than I thought. Remember, it's two years minimum at Pax River if this assignment goes. You know that?"

"Yes."

"And if O'Hara gets transferred somewhere else you're still there, you know that?"

"How did you know it was Rusty?"

"Like adding two and two. Congratulations, Allison."

* * *

The detailer called three days later. Less than an hour afterward, she called Rusty.

"You did *what?*" he said.

"My orders are to fly the station S-3 at Pax River."

"Allison, Allison, how will you ever get a fleet seat from that job? Why didn't you ask me first?"

"You'd say what you just said. Besides, the decision's mine anyway."

"I know how much flying an F-14 means to you."

"And I know how much test pilot school means to you, and how hard it is to get through. You can use some help."

He was silent for a few seconds.

"You really don't play games, do you, sailor?"

"No guts, no Air Medal, sailor," she replied.

When Allison flew into Pax River the following weekend with another student on a cross-country, Rusty waited on the ramp. He started toward her, noticing the new pilot. He took her hand and waited until the unfamiliar ensign got his gear together.

After the student headed for Base Ops, Rusty walked her behind the T-2's fuselage and kissed her fiercely. She wrapped her arms around him, her face warm and flushed. She wanted to be somewhere, anywhere, alone with him now.

"I picked up something to dress up your drab-looking flight suit, sailor," he said.

Rusty pulled a small box from his pocket and flipped up the top. A sparkling one-carat, blue-white diamond in a gold setting stared up at her.

"You can only have this if you'll wear the one that goes with it," he said. "Better make up your mind. Allison O'Hara doesn't sound that bad," he added.

"It's beautiful," she said. She looked up at him and kissed him again. "You drive a hard bargain, Rusty, but I think I can handle it."

She crushed him to her, closed her eyes, and wasn't sure when she'd ever let go. Words were useless.

The road had been long from the ramp at Norfolk when she was ten, from the selection board for flight school, even from the day she had first met him a few months ago. Any number of things could have changed this day, but she hadn't let them. Now no one, or no thing, not even the United States Navy or its big, powerful fighter aircraft, would change the rest, either.